Tales from Two Pockets

Tales
From Two Pockets

by

Karel Čapek

Translated from the Czech by
Paul Selver

London
GEORGE ALLEN & UNWIN LTD
RUSKIN HOUSE · MUSEUM STREET

FIRST PUBLISHED IN GREAT BRITAIN IN 1932
SECOND IMPRESSION 1943
THIRD IMPRESSION 1967

PRINTED IN GREAT BRITAIN
BY PHOTOLITHOGRAPHY
UNWIN BROTHERS LIMITED
WOKING AND LONDON

Contents

★　★　★

Tales from one Pocket

Tales from the other Pocket

Acknowledgments

Some of these stories first appeared in English in various periodicals—the *Manchester Guardian*, the *London Mercury*, *Time and Tide*, the *Spectator*, *Harper's Bazaar*, and *Reynolds's Newspaper*,—and to the editors and proprietors of these publications the usual courtesies are due.

Tales from one Pocket

* * *

The Stolen Papers—139/vii Sect. C.

* * *

AT THREE o'clock in the morning the telephone at garrison headquarters gave a sudden whirr :

" This is Colonel Hampl of the General Staff. Send two military policemen to me at once. And tell Lieutenant-Colonel Vrzal, he's in the Intelligence Department, yes, of course, oh, that's nothing to do with you, tell him to come here at once. Yes, now at this very moment. Yes, by car. But be quick about it, for Heaven's sake."

And the speaker rang off.

An hour later Lieutenant-Colonel Vrzal was on the spot. It was a long way out, somewhere in the garden suburb. He was received by a middle-aged gentleman with a very worried look and in mufti, or rather, in shirt and trousers.

" I say, I'm in a devil of a mess. Just sit down, will you ? It's a confounded, blasted, damned, rotten, sickening business. A hell of a fix to be in, I can tell you. It's like this : The day before yesterday the chief of the General Staff gave me some papers and said : *Hampl, you'd better work on this at home. The fewer people who know about it, the better. Mum's the word in the office. Now then, off you go, take a few days' leave and do the job at home. But keep your wits about you. All right.*"

" What papers were they ? " inquired Lieutenant-Colonel Vrzal.

Colonel Hampl hesitated.

" Well," he said, " as a matter of fact, they were from Section C."

" Aha ! " observed Lieutenant-Colonel Vrzal, and began to look exceedingly grave. " Go on."

5

" Well now, look here," said the crestfallen colonel. " Yesterday I was busy on the job all day. But then I wondered what in the name of goodness I was to do with the damned thing at night. No use putting it into a drawer. I haven't got a safe. And if anyone knew that it was in my hands, there'd be the devil to pay. Well, for the first night I shoved it in my bed under the mattress and by the morning it was crumpled all out of shape, as if an elephant had been trampling on it."

" I bet it was," said Lieutenant-Colonel Vrzal.

" Well, it can't be helped," sighed the colonel. " My wife's even stouter than I am. Anyway, the next night my wife suggested we should put the papers into a macaroni-tin and keep it in the pantry during the night. *I'll lock the pantry for the night, and look after the key*, said my wife. You see we've got one of those shockingly fat servant-girls who're always asleep. *Nobody's going to look for it in the pantry, are they?* said my wife. Very well, then. I thought it was a good idea."

" Has your pantry got double or single windows ? " Lieutenant-Colonel Vrzal interrupted him.

" Confound it all," burst forth the colonel, " I never thought of that. Single windows! I completely forgot to look at the windows. Damn and blast the confounded thing ! "

" Well, go on," the lieutenant-colonel urged him.

" That's about all there is to tell. At two in the morning my wife heard the servant-girl screaming down below. She went to ask what was the matter, and Mary yelled out : *There's a burglar in the pantry*. My wife ran for the key and to fetch me, I rushed down into the pantry with a pistol, and damn and blast it all ! the window in the pantry had been opened with a thingumabob, a crowbar, and the tin box with the papers was gone. And the burglar was gone, too. That's the lot," said the colonel with a sigh.

Lieutenant-Colonel Vrzal drummed on the table with his fingers.

" And did anybody know you'd got these papers at home ? "

The unhappy colonel shrugged his shoulders.

" I don't know. My dear fellow, those spies manage to sniff out everything, the dirty crooks." But then he remembered what Lieutenant-Colonel Vrzal's particular job was and was covered with confusion. " That is, what I mean to say is, they're jolly smart fellows," he corrected himself feebly. " But I never told a soul, I give you my word I didn't. Why," he added triumphantly, " nobody could have known I put the papers into the macaroni-tin."

" And where were you when you put them in the tin ? " asked the lieutenant-colonel casually.

" Here, at this table."

" Whereabouts was the tin then ? "

" Let's see now," reflected the colonel. " I was sitting here and I had the tin right in front of me."

The lieutenant-colonel leaned against the table and gazed dreamily out of the window. In the dewy daybreak the outlines of a grey and red villa stood out opposite.

" Who lives there ? " he asked wearily.

The colonel banged his fist on the table.

" God damn it all, I never thought of that ! Let's see now, there's a Jew living there, a bank manager or something. Confound the thing, now I see it all. Vrzal, it strikes me that we've got a clue."

" I'd like to have a look at that pantry," said the lieutenant-colonel evasively.

" Come along, then. This way, this way," said the colonel, leading him eagerly. " Here it is. The box was on that top shelf. Mary," bellowed the colonel, " what are you staring at ? Go to the attic or else into the cellar."

The lieutenant-colonel took off his gloves and swung himself up to the window, which was rather high.

" Prised open with a chisel," he said, inspecting the window. " The window-frame's made of soft wood, though. Any schoolboy could split it apart."

" Confound the thing ! " The colonel was taken aback. " Confound the people, what do they mean by making such rotten windows."

Outside, in front of the grating, two soldiers were in attendance.

" Is that the military police ? " inquired Lieutenant-Colonel Vrzal. " That's right. I'll just have a look outside. By the way, if I were you I'd stay at home until further orders."

" Oh, of course," agreed the colonel. " But what for ? "

" So as to be at hand, in case—— Those two soldiers will stay here, of course."

The colonel snorted and then gulped something down.

" I see. Won't you have some coffee ? My wife will make you some."

" There's no time for that now," said the lieutenant-colonel curtly. " Of course, you won't breathe a word to anyone about these stolen papers, except when . . . when you're sent for. And there's one more thing : tell the servant-girl that the burglar only stole some jam."

" But I say," exclaimed the colonel in despair, " you're going to find those papers, aren't you ? "

" I'm going to look for them," said the lieutenant-colonel, and clicked his heels together in the prescribed manner.

All that morning Colonel Hampl moved about like a bundle of misery. There were moments when in his mind's eye he saw two officers coming to arrest him ; there were other moments when he tried to imagine what Lieutenant-

Colonel Vrzal was up to and how he would set in motion the vast and hidden mechanism of the military intelligence service. He pictured to himself how scared the general staff would be, and he groaned.

" Karlous," said his wife to him for the twentieth time (to be on the safe side she had hidden his revolver in the servant-girl's trunk at an early stage in the proceedings), " wouldn't you like something to eat ? "

" For God's sake leave me alone ! " snarled the colonel. " I expect it was that Jew opposite who spotted me."

His wife sighed and went off into the kitchen to have a good cry.

At this moment the bell rang. The colonel stood up and pulled himself together. He would be strictly soldier-like in his reception of the officers who were coming to arrest him. (He wondered distractedly who they were likely to be.) But instead of the officers a sandy little man entered with a billycock hat in his hand and showed the colonel a set of teeth like a squirrel's.

" Beg your pardon, sir, but my name's Pistora and I'm from the police-station here."

" What do you want ? " demanded the colonel explosively, as with a casual movement he changed over from attention to at ease.

" I hear as how your pantry's been burgled," said Mr. Pistora, with a toothy grin and a slightly confidential air. " So I just came along."

" And what's it got to do with you ? " barked the colonel.

" Beg your pardon, sir," beamed Mr. Pistora, " but this here's my beat, see ? Your servant-girl, she was telling them this morning at the baker's that your pantry's been burgled, so I says to the inspector, I says, I'll just run along there, see ? "

" It's not worth troubling about," objected the colonel

testily. " They only took—er—a tin of macaroni.
You may as well let the matter slide."

" It's funny," observed Mr. Pistora, " that they didn't
collar more than that."

" Yes, it's very funny," said the colonel sourly. " But
there's no need for you to bother about it."

" I expect someone disturbed 'em," said Mr. Pistora in a
sudden burst of brightness.

" Well, good day," snapped the colonel.

" Beg your pardon, sir," said Mr. Pistora with a mistrustful
smile, " but I've got to have a look at that there pantry
first, sir."

The colonel was about to let himself go, but then he sub-
mitted to his plight.

" Come along then," he said with distaste, and led the
little man to the pantry.

Mr. Pistora gazed delightedly round the poky little room.

" Oh, yes," he said in a satisfied tone, " the window's been
forced open with a chisel. That must have been Pepek or
Andrlik."

" What do you mean ? " asked the colonel sharply.

" Why, it was Pepek or Andrlik who done that. But I
reckon that Pepek's doing time. If the glass had only been
pushed out, it might have been Dundr, Lojza, Novak,
Hosicka, or Kliment. But this here was one of Andrlik's jobs."

" You seem very cocksure about it," growled the colonel.

" You don't think there's anybody new round here after
pantries ? " said Mr. Pistora with sudden gravity. " I don't
reckon it's likely. There's Mertl who opens windows with
chisels too, but then he never goes after pantries, sir, he
don't. What he does is to get through the closet into the
house, and all he takes is linen." Mr. Pistora showed his
squirrelly teeth. " Well, I reckon I'll have a squint at
Andrlik."

" Remember me to him," fumed the colonel. It's incredible, he brooded, when he was again left to his dismal reflections, what utter duffers the police are. If they'd only look for some finger-prints or foot-marks—that'd be all right, that's something like a method. But the idiotic way they go about it,—how on earth can they be expected to tackle international espionage ? I only wish I knew what Vrzal is up to.

The colonel could not resist the temptation to ring up Lieutenant-Colonel Vrzal. After half an hour's raging he managed to get through to him. " Hallo ! " he exclaimed in honeyed tones. " This is Hampl speaking. I say, how much have you—I know you mustn't talk about it, but I only—I know, but if you could just tell me whether there's any—Good heavens, nothing yet ?—I know it's a difficult case, but—— I say, Vrzal, just a moment. It struck me I might offer a reward of ten thousand crowns out of my own pocket, of course, to anyone who nabs the thief. That's all I've got, but you know what it'd mean to me, if—— Yes, I know, but quite privately—— Why, yes, just my private affair, it couldn't be done officially. Or it could be divided among the detectives, eh ? Oh, of course, you're not supposed to know about it, but if you just sort of dropped a hint to those chaps that Colonel Hampl has promised ten thousand. Right you are, then, your sergeant can mention it. You might see to it, old fellow. Excuse me for troubling you. Thanks very much."

This bountiful resolution brought Colonel Hampl a slight relief. It made him feel that now he himself had at least some share in tracking down the confounded, rascally spy. He lay down on the sofa, because he was tired after all the excitement and pictured to himself how a hundred, two hundred, three hundred men (they were all sandy and showed their squirrelly teeth like Mr. Pistora) were searching trains, stopping motor-cars which raced towards the frontier, lying in wait for their prey at street-corners, and suddenly appearing on the scene with the words : *In the name of the law, come with me and hold your tongue.* Then he dreamt that he was sitting for an examination in ballistics at the military academy, moaned loudly and woke up in a sweat. There was a ring at the bell.

Colonel Hampl jumped up and tried to straighten out his thoughts. In the doorway appeared Mr. Pistora's squirrelly teeth.

" Well, here I am again," remarked the squirrelly teeth. " It was him all right, sir."

" Who ? " inquired the colonel, attempting to comprehend.

" Why, Andrlik, of course," said Mr. Pistora in such surprise that he stopped showing his teeth. " Who else could it have been ? Pepek's doing time, see ? "

" But what do you keep trotting out this chap Andrlik for ? " growled the colonel testily.

Mr. Pistora's small bright eyes goggled.

" Why, it was him who stole the macaroni from your pantry," he said with mild emphasis. " They've got him in custody at the police-station. Beg your pardon, sir, but I just come to ask—you see, this here Andrlik says there wasn't any macaroni in that box, but only some pieces of paper. I was just wondering, like, whether it was true or not."

" Look here," exclaimed the colonel breathlessly, " where are those pieces of paper ? "

" In my pocket." Mr. Pistora showed his teeth. " Where the——? " He fumbled in his alpaca jacket. " —Ah. Is this yours ? "

The colonel dragged from his hand the precious, crumpled papers No. 139/vii, Sect. C. Tears of relief welled up in his eyes. " You're a brick and no mistake," he murmured.

" I'm more obliged to you than I can say. My dear," he gave a sudden yell, " just step this way, will you. Here's superintendent, er, inspector, er——"

" Police Constable Pistora," said the little man, showing his dentures with the utmost satisfaction.

" Well, he's found those stolen papers already," exulted the colonel. " Come along, my dear, bring glasses and some brandy. Mr. Pistora, I'd like to . . . but I don't quite know how . . . what I mean is . . . Have a drink, Mr. Pistora."

" Why, that was nothing at all," said Mr. Pistora with a toothy smile. " This liquor's got some bite in it, sir. Oh, and that there box, ma'am, is at the police-station."

" Box be damned ! " thundered the colonel blissfully. " My dear Mr. Pistora, it was wonderful how quickly you found those papers. Here's my respects, Mr. Pistora."

" Same to you, sir," said Mr. Pistora respectfully. " Good Lord, that's nothing at all. When a pantry's been broke open, we goes after Andrlik or Pepek, but Pepek's doing two months at present. If it's a top floor, it lays between Pisecky, Tondera with the lame leg, Kaner, Zima, and Houska."

" Well, I never ! " said the colonel in astonishment. " And look here, suppose it was a case of spying, what about that ? Your health, Mr. Pistora."

" Same to you, sir. Spying, sir, oh, that ain't in our line. But brass hooks, that's Cenek or Pinkus, copper-wire, there's only one bloke goes in for that and his name's Tousek, and if it's lead piping, it's bound to be Hanousek, Buchta, or Slesinger. Yes, sir, all that's a dead cert for us. And safe-breakers, we got them taped from all over the country. There's—hic—there's twenty-seven of 'em, but six are in quod."

" Serve 'em right," declared the colonel blood-thirstily. " Mr. Pistora, drink up."

" Thanks very much, sir," said Mr. Pistora, " but I ain't much of a drinker. Well, here's my best respects, sir. Them there—hic—them there crooks, they ain't what you'd call intelligent, sir. Each of 'em's just got one little stunt, like, and he keeps to it till we collars him again. Like that chap Andrlik : *Aha*, he says, as soon as ever he'd clapped eyes on me, *that's Mr. Pistora about that there pantry. Mr. Pistora, it ain't worth while, all I found in that box was some pieces of paper. I had to hop it before I could collar anything. You come along with me, I says to him, You'll get at least a year for this, you damn fool.*"

" A year's imprisonment," remarked Colonel Hampl compassionately. " Isn't that rather a lot ? "

" Why, that's burglarious entry, sir," and Mr. Pistora showed his teeth. " Well, much obliged to you, sir. I've got to see about a shop-front, now. It's either Klecka or Rudl. And if you should want anything, just you ask at the police-station. All you got to do is to mention me—Pistora's the name, sir."

" By the way," said the colonel, " if you—hm—for this little job—what I mean to say, those pieces of paper weren't anything special, but—I'd be sorry to lose them, do you see ? Well, supposing you just took this for the job," he said hastily, and thrust a fifty-crown note into Mr. Pistora's hand.

Mr. Pistora became quite solemn with surprise and emotion. " There wasn't any need for that," he said, rapidly slipping his hand with the bank-note into his pocket. " That wasn't anything. Well, much obliged to you, sir. And if you should want anything——"

" So I gave him fifty crowns," said Colonel Hampl to his wife. " Twenty would have been quite enough for a booby of that sort, but——" The colonel waved his hand magnanimously " —after all, he did find those confounded papers."

The Clairvoyant

★　　★　　★

"YOU KNOW, Dr. Klapka," quoth Mr. Janowitz, "it's not so easy to take me in. I'm not a Jew for nothing. But what that fellow does is quite beyond me. It's not what you'd call graphology, it's—well, I don't know what it is. Now just let me tell you about it : You give him a manuscript in an unsealed envelope ; he doesn't even look at it, but just shoves his fingers into the envelope and passes them over the writing ; his mouth sort of twitches as if something was hurting him, and after a while be begins to tell you the character of the writer—really, you'd be flabbergasted, the way he gets every detail right. Why, I handed him an envelope with a letter inside it from old Weinberger, and he found out everything about the old boy, even that he'd got diabetes and that he was going bankrupt. What do you think of that ? "

" Nothing," said Dr. Klapka dryly (he was the public prosecutor). " It's possible that he knows old Weinberger."

" But he never even saw the writing," retorted Mr. Janowitz excitedly. " He says that each handwriting gives off a fluid of its own and it can be detected with absolute accuracy by the sense of touch. He says it works by pure physics, just like wireless. There's no fraud about it, though. This Prince Karadagh doesn't do it for money. He belongs to a very old family from Baku, so a Russian told me. But don't take my word for it, come and have a look for yourself. He'll be at my place this evening. You must come round."

" Look here, Mr. Janowitz," said the public prosecutor, " that's all very fine, but I only believe fifty per cent. of what

I hear where foreigners are concerned, especially when I don't know how they make their living. Where Russians are concerned, the percentage is smaller still, and with these fakir chaps least of all. But when on top of everything else the man's supposed to be a prince, I don't believe a word of what he says. Where did you say he learnt this stuff ? Oh yes, in Persia. Really, Mr. Janowitz, you can't expect me to swallow that. All these Oriental yarns are humbug."

" But this young man explains it on absolutely scientific lines," protested Mr. Janowitz. " There's no magic, and no secret forces, but you can take my word for it that his method's strictly scientific."

" That's bigger humbug still," remarked the public prosecutor reproachfully. " I'm surprised at you, Mr. Janowitz. You've managed to get along all your life without any strictly scientific methods, and now you let them be foisted off on you. Hang it ! if there was anything in this, it would have been heard of long ago, wouldn't it ? "

" Well, I don't know," observed Mr. Janowitz, rather waveringly, " but with my own eyes I saw him find out all about old Weinberger. I tell you, it was a sheer stroke of genius ! Now, look here, you just come along and have a look for yourself. If it's a fraud, why, you're bound to see through it. That's your job. Nobody's going to bamboozle you."

" Hardly, I think," said the public prosecutor modestly. " All right, then, I'll come along, Mr. Janowitz, but only so that I can keep a sharp watch on this prodigy of yours. It's awful how gullible the people here are. But you mustn't tell him who I am. Just you wait, I'll give him a manuscript in an envelope to read that'll be a tough nut for him to crack. And I bet you I'll prove he's a fraud."

You must know that Dr. Klapka was acting as public

prosecutor in the forthcoming trial of Hugo Muller on a charge of wilful murder. Mr. Hugo Muller, a business man and a millionaire, was accused of having drowned his younger brother, Otto, in a pond, after having insured his life for a large sum of money. Moreover, he was suspected of having made away with a sweetheart of his, some years previously, but there was no chance of proving that. It was one of those big trials which the public prosecutor was anxious to make the most of, and he had been studying the documentary material with all that zeal and insight which had made him the most formidable of public prosecutors. The case was not all plain sailing ; the public prosecutor would have given a good deal for a single direct piece of evidence, but as things were, he had to rely on his gift of the gab to obtain from the jury a verdict against Mr. Muller. For you must understand that this is an affair of honour for a public prosecutor.

That evening Mr. Janowitz was a wee bit agitated. " This is Prince Karadagh "—he performed the introduction in muffled tones. " Dr. Klapka. We may as well make a start, eh ? "

The public prosecutor gazed searchingly at the exotic creature. He was a slender young man with glasses, with the face of a Tibetan monk and the delicate hands of a pickpocket. " The man's a crook," decided the public prosecutor briefly.

" Mr. Karadagh," stammered Mr. Janowitz, " here at this table. The mineral water's already here. Just light this table-lamp. We'll switch off the chandelier, so that it shan't disturb you. That's it. Now then, gentlemen, silence, please. Mr.—er—Mr. Klapka here will oblige with a manuscript. Perhaps Mr. Karadagh wouldn't mind——"

The public prosecutor gave a brief cough and sat down where he could get the best view of the clairvoyant. " Here's the manuscript," he said, and took an unsealed envelope from his breast pocket. "Allow me."

"Thank you," said the clairvoyant wearily, when he took the envelope and with closed eyes turned it over with his finger-tips. "Strange," he muttered, and swallowed a gulp of water. Then he thrust his thin fingers into the envelope and shuddered; it looked as if his sallow face went paler still.

The room was so quiet that Mr. Janowitz could be heard wheezing; for Mr. Janowitz had a goitre.

Prince Karadagh's thin lips quivered and twisted, as if he were squeezing red-hot iron between his fingers, and sweat came out on his forehead. "This is more than I can stand," he hissed tensely, withdrew his fingers from the envelope, wiped them on his handkerchief and passed them for a moment over the tablecloth, as if he were whetting a knife. Whereupon he again sipped excitedly at the water and cautiously took the envelope between his fingers.

"The man who wrote that—" he began listlessly—"the man who wrote that——This shows great strength, but the kind of strength which—" (here he was evidently searching for a word)—"which watches. The way he watches is awful," he exclaimed, and dropped the envelope on to the table. "I should not like to have that man for my enemy."

"Why?" the public prosecutor could not help asking. "Has he done anything wrong?"

"Do not ask me," said the clairvoyant. "Every question gives a hint. I only know that he would stick at nothing; he is capable of great and terrible deeds. This shows enormous will-power, craving for success, for money. This man would not let a man's life stand in his way. No, he is no ordinary criminal; the tiger is no criminal; the tiger is a lord of creation. This man is incapable of a mean action, but he thinks that he rules over the lives of men. Once he is out for blood, he looks upon men only as so much prey. Then he kills them."

" Beyond good and evil," muttered the public prosecutor in evident agreement.

" Those are only words," said Prince Karadagh. " Nobody is beyond good and evil. This man has precise moral ideas of his own. He is not in debt to anyone, he does not steal, he does not lie ; if he kills, he does so as if he were checkmating his opponent at chess. That is his game, but he plays it properly." The clairvoyant laboriously wrinkled his forehead. " I do not know what this is. I see a large pond with a motor-boat on it."

" And what else ? " gasped the public prosecutor with bated breath.

" I can see nothing else. It is all misty. It is so strangely misty in contrast to his cruel and relentless will to get his prey. But there is no passion about it, only reason. Absolutely rational deliberation. Just as when a sum or a technical problem is being worked out. No, this man can never feel any self-reproach. He is too self-confident, too sure of himself for that ; he need not fear any qualms of conscience. He strikes me as being a man who looks down on everything ; he is extremely conceited and self-satisfied ; he is pleased that people are afraid of him." The clairvoyant sipped at the water. " But he is also a mountebank. At bottom an opportunist, who acts a part. He is anxious to astound the world by his deeds. No more. I am tired. I do not like him."

" I say, Janowitz," declared the public prosecutor excitedly, " that clairvoyant of yours is really a marvel. The description he gave was perfect. A strong and ruthless man, who regards people only as so much prey ; who knows every trick in the game ; a clever fellow who by sheer brain-work gets a job all mapped out beforehand ; a man of his word and at the same time a mountebank. I tell you, Janowitz, this chap Karadagh hit him off to a T."

" There you are," said Mr. Janowitz in a gratified tone. " Didn't I tell you so ? That was a letter from Schlieffen, of Schlieffen & Co., wasn't it ? "

" Good Lord, no ! " exclaimed the public prosecutor. " Why, that was a letter from a murderer."

" You don't say so," marvelled Mr. Janowitz, " and I thought that it was Schlieffen, the textile man. He's a thorough-paced crook, is Schlieffen."

" No, that was a letter from Hugo Muller, who murdered his brother. Did you notice how the clairvoyant mentioned a boat on a pond ? That was the boat that Muller threw his brother out of into the water."

" You don't say so," said Mr. Janowitz in tones of amazement. " Just fancy that now ! He must be something quite out of the way."

" Most decidedly," agreed the public prosecutor. " Just the way he hit off Muller's character and the motives for his act, why, it's nothing short of prodigious, Mr. Janowitz. Why, I myself couldn't have got at the truth about Muller with such an accuracy of detail. And this clairvoyant fellow does it just by touch, from a few lines of one of Muller's letters. There's something in it, Mr. Janowitz. There must be a special sort of fluid or something in people's handwriting."

" What did I tell you ? " said Mr. Janowitz gloatingly. " By the way, I've never seen a murderer's handwriting, I wonder if you'd mind——"

" With pleasure," said the public prosecutor, and took the envelope out of his pocket. " As a matter of fact, it's a very interesting letter," he added, removing the paper from the envelope. But suddenly he changed colour. " Oh, Mr.

Janowitz, I'm sorry, but——" he blurted out in an uneasy kind of way. " You see, this letter is one of the documents in the case and I—I mustn't show it to you. I hope you don't mind."

A moment later the public prosecutor was dashing along home, without even noticing that it was raining. What a fool I am, he said to himself bitterly, what a lunatic, how could such a thing ever happen to me ? What an idiot I am ! In my hurry I must have mistaken Muller's letter in the file for my own notes on the case and that's how I came to put them in this envelope. What a lunatic I am ! So that was my handwriting ! A pretty business, upon my word ! Just you wait, you swindler. I've got my eye on you.

But after all, the public prosecutor began to comfort himself. On the whole it wasn't so bad, what he said. Great strength ; enormous will-power, mark you ; I am incapable of a mean action ; I have moral ideas of my own—it's really all quite complimentary. I can never feel any self-reproach? Well, thank goodness, I have no need to ; I do my duty. And what he said about sheer brain-work was quite true. But he was wrong about the mountebank. No, it's nothing but a swindle after all.

Suddenly he stopped. Why, of course, he said to himself, what the clairvoyant told us would apply equally well to anyone else. It was just a string of general remarks. Every man is a bit of a mountebank and opportunist. That's the trick of it all : to put things in such a way as to make everyone recognize himself. That's how it's done, decided the public prosecutor, and opening his umbrella he moved on towards home with a regular and energetic stride.

" Great heavens ! " lamented the president of the court, removing his robes, " it's already seven o'clock. How these cases do drag on ! Well, seeing that the public prosecutor spoke for two hours on end—though I must say, he did the trick all right. To get a verdict of guilty on such weak evidence as that, why, that's what you might call a clever bit of work. Still, with juries you never can tell. All the same, that was a neat speech of his," remarked the president, washing his hands, " specially the way he described Muller's character—that was nothing short of a finished portrait. You know it was enough to make anyone shudder when he was enlarging on how monstrous and inhuman the murderer must be. Do you remember when he said: He is no ordinary criminal ; he is incapable of a mean action, he does not lie or steal ; but if he murders a man, he does it as calmly as if he were checkmating his opponent at chess. He does not murder as the result of passion, but with cool rational deliberation, as if he were working out a sum or a technical problem. That was well put, you know. And then again : Once he is out after blood, he looks upon men only as so much prey. You know, what he said about a tiger was a bit melodramatic, but the jury liked it immensely."

" And then, too," added the assistant judge, " when he said : This murderer assuredly can never feel any self-reproach ; he is so self-satisfied, so sure of himself—he need never fear any qualms of conscience."

" Or again that clever bit of pyschological reasoning," continued the president, wiping his hands on the towel, " that he is a mountebank and a *poseur* who would like to astound the world with his deeds."

" Oh, yes," agreed the assistant judge. " Klapka's a dangerous man to be up against."

" Just fancy, a unanimous verdict of guilty against Hugo Muller ! " exclaimed the president. " Who would have believed it possible ! Yet Klapka managed it all right. He looks on it as a game of chess or a hunting-party. That's the way he gets his teeth into every case he takes up. I tell you, I shouldn't like to have him for an enemy."

" Yes," said the assistant judge, " he fairly gloats over the idea that people are afraid of him."

" He's a bit self-satisfied," said the worthy president reflectively. " But he's got enormous will-power, he just craves for success. A man of great strength, but—— " the president could not find the right word. " Well, let's go and get a bite of food."

The Secrets of Handwriting

★ ★ ★

"RUBNER," said the editor, "just go and have a look at Jensen, that graphologist fellow. He's giving a show this evening for representatives of the Press. He's supposed to be one of the marvels of the age. After you've been, let me have fifteen lines about it."

"Right you are," grunted Rubner, with the scanty willingness proper to a man receiving a job of work.

"And keep your eyes open for any signs of fraud," the editor urged. "Check his results yourself, if possible. That's why I'm sending an experienced man like you there."

" . . . so then, gentlemen, these are the main principles of scientific, or to put it more accurately, psychometric graphology." That was how Jensen, the graphologist, concluded his theoretical exposition that evening to representatives of the Press. "As you see, a whole system is constructed upon purely experimental laws ; but, to be sure, the practical application of these exact methods is so exceedingly complicated that at this single lecture I cannot demonstrate it in any detail. I will limit myself to giving a practical analysis of two or three specimens of handwriting without theoretically explaining to you my whole procedure ; unfortunately we have not enough time for that to-day. Would one of the gentlemen present kindly let me have a manuscript ? "

Rubner, who had been waiting for this, immediately handed the great Jensen a sheet of paper covered with writing. Jensen put on his magicianly spectacles and looked at the script.

" Aha, a woman's hand," he smirked. " Men's handwriting is generally more expressive and interesting, but never mind——" He mumbled something, staring attentively at the sheet of paper. " Hm, hm," he said every now and then, and shook his head ; there was deep stillness.

" May I ask if this was written by . . . by someone with whom you are on close terms ? " the graphologist suddenly asked.

" No, rather not," protested Rubner hastily.

" All the better," said the great Jensen. " Well now, this woman tells lies. That is the first impression which this handwriting produces ; she tells lies, by force of habit ; she tells lies as a matter of course. Moreover, her standard of intelligence is extremely low ; an educated man would not find much to talk to her about. She is inordinately sensual ; her writing displays what are known as obese forms. And she is shockingly untidy ; what her surroundings can look like—well, words fail me ! Those are the primary traits which I mentioned to you just now. The first thing which you discover about a person are his habits, that is, the peculiarities which express themselves outwardly, *ipso facto*, in a purely mechanical manner. The real psychological analysis only begins with those peculiarities which the person in question denies or suppresses, because otherwise he would give himself away to those around him. Now for example," he said, placing his finger on the tip of his nose, " this particular person would be hardly likely to admit to anyone what she really thinks. She is superficial, but superficial in a twofold sense : she displays herself superficially, she has many commonplace interests, but she uses all this merely to conceal what she really thinks ; and this hidden ego is preposterously banal. I am inclined to describe it as depravity which is at the beck and call of mental sloth. Just look here, for instance : the writing is sensual to an appalling degree—that's also a sign of extravagance—and at the same time it is so blatantly respectable ; this person is too fond of her comfort to go out looking for adventures of a certain sort ; of course, when a chance comes her way—however, we're not concerned with that.   She is exceedingly slothful and, at the same time, an awful chatterbox ; when she does do anything, she'll talk about it till one is sick and tired of hearing her voice.   She is too much taken up with herself ; it is evident that she cares for nobody ; it is merely for the sake of her own comfort that she clings to somebody and wants to make him believe she loves him and worries about him no end.   She is one of those women who will reduce any man to a flabby-minded state ; he just lapses into it through sheer boredom, as a result of her everlasting chatter, and the whole abject blatancy of it.   Just notice the way she writes the beginnings of words, and especially of sentences ; it's all so flamboyant and flimsy.   The good woman wants to rule the roost, and she does ; but there's no energy about it all, only a kind of false importance and a lot of fussiness ; and, when the need for it arises, the basest form of tyranny— I mean the tyranny of tears.   This is curious ; after each flourish you can see a marked droop, indicating sheer faint-heartedness ; she wants to hold something in check, there's something she's constantly afraid of—most likely she's anxious to keep something to herself which might endanger her material comfort ; it must be something very unpleasant and carefully concealed—hm—I'm not quite sure ; it may be something in her past.   Not until she has overcome this re-pression does she recover enough energy, or rather force of habit, to finish the word in conventional style—of course, with a self-satisfied and straggling flourish at the end ; by that time her self-confidence is beginning to return to her. There you have in analysis the first impression of mendacity. It shows you, gentlemen, at the same time, how a detailed analysis must finally confirm the first general impression which is somewhat intuitive ; this final agreement I call methodical verification. I have mentioned her low standard of intelligence, but this low standard is not due to primitive development, but to a lack of inner harmony. The handwriting is pretentious, she tries to make it look neater than it really is, but she does so in paltry details. She is a person who makes a point of being more or less accurate over trifles. She carefully dots her *i*'s, but in matters of real importance she is slipshod, without discipline, without moral principles, a slattern, pure and simple. It is the commas which are the most startling feature of her handwriting, which normally tends to slope towards the right, while the commas are placed in the opposite direction. That produces a queer effect, like a stab in the back. There is something treacherous and cunning about it. To put the matter figuratively, I would say that she is capable of stabbing anyone from behind, but she would not do it because of her slothful disposition and her lack of imagination. I think that's about all. Has anyone got another, more interesting specimen of handwriting ? "

That evening Rubner went home with a face as black as thunder.

" So you're back at last," said Mrs. Rubner. " Have you had anything to eat yet ? "

Rubner scowled at her. " You're beginning again, are you ? " he snarled.

Mrs. Rubner raised her eyebrows in surprise. " What do you mean, I'm beginning again ? I'm only asking you if you've had anything to eat yet."

" There you are," said Rubner with disgust. " Of course, the only thing you can talk about is food. All your interests are commonplace. It's so degrading, this everlasting chatter, this blatancy and dullness——" Rubner sighed and waved his hand despairingly. " Yes, that's how men get reduced to a flabby-minded state."

Mrs. Rubner laid her sewing in her lap and looked at him attentively. " Franc," she said anxiously, " has something unpleasant happened to you ? "

" Aha ! " Rubner blurted out viciously. " You're worrying about me again, are you ? Now then, don't imagine you can take me in in that way. Oh, no, sooner or later a man sees through all that mendacity ; sooner or later he realizes that someone is clinging to him just for their own comfort . . . and out of sheer sensuality. Bah ! " bellowed Rubner, " it's enough to make anyone shudder."

Mrs. Rubner shook her head and was about to say something, but she tightened her lips and began to sew rapidly. There was silence.

" This is a fine home," hissed Rubner after a while and stared about him with a heavy eye. " All untidy and slovenly—— Of course, over trifles there's a lot of fuss made about tidiness and accuracy—but where more important matters are concerned—— What are these rags doing here ? "

" I'm mending your shirts," gasped Mrs. Rubner.

" Mending shirts, eh ? " sneered Rubner. " Fancy that now, mending shirts ! Of course, everyone must know about it, mustn't they ? Half the day has to be spent in letting people know that somebody's mending shirts. All this fussing about and putting on airs ! And you think that because of that you're going to rule the roost. Well, it's going to stop, let me tell you ! "

" Franc," gasped Mrs. Rubner, " have I done you any harm ? "

" How do I know ? " snapped Rubner. " I don't know what you've been doing ; I don't know what you're thinking about and what you've got up your sleeve ; I know nothing about you, nothing whatever, because you damn well keep back what's inside you. Why, I don't even know what sort of a life you led before I met you."

"Now look here," Mrs. Rubner burst forth, "that's the last straw. If you say another word——" She controlled herself by a supreme effort. "Darling," she said with a shudder, "what's happened to you?"

"Aha!" exclaimed Rubner triumphantly. "There you are! What were you so scared about? I suppose in case something might come out that would be likely to upset the cosy life you're leading, eh? I know all about it. Now and then, though she has it all her own way, she finds a chance to have some fun on the quiet, doesn't she?"

Mrs. Rubner sat there as if turned to stone. "Darling," she gulped, swallowing her sobs, "if you're got anything against me, why, for goodness' sake, say it straight out."

"Nothing whatever," quoth Rubner with tremendous irony. "Why, what an idea! I've got nothing whatever against you. It's a matter of no consequence if a man has a wife without any sense of order, without morals, a wife who is deceitful, untidy, vulgar, lazy, extravagant, and appallingly sensual! And on top of all that, such a low standard of—"

Mrs. Rubner burst out sobbing. She stood up, and let her sewing fall on the floor.

"Stop that," her husband yelled scornfully, "that's the basest form of tyranny—the tyranny of tears."

But Mrs. Rubner was no longer listening, for, choking with spasms of weeping, she had rushed into her bedroom.

Rubner gave a hollow cackle and thrust his head through the doorway. "You could stab a man in the back," he shouted, "only you're too fond of your comfort even to do that!"

The next evening Rubner dropped into his favourite

eating-house. " I've just been reading in your paper here,"
Mr. Plečka welcomed him, looking over the top of his glasses,
" the way they're cracking up Jensen, that handwriting
chap. Is there anything in it ? "

" Yes, plenty," said Mr. Rubner. " Well, Mr. Jančík, let
me have a cut from the joint, but see it isn't tough. Oh
yes, he's a marvel, Jensen is. I saw him yesterday. He'll
analyse your handwriting for you scientifically."

" Then it's a fraud," remarked Mr. Plečka. " Yes, sir,
I'll believe in anything except science. Now take these here
vitamins. Before there was such a thing as vitamins, you at
least knew what you was eating. But now you can't tell.
Now all you've got in a joint is what they call vital factors,
and Lord knows what they are. It's all damn rot ! "
declared Mr. Plečka with disgust.

" This is a different thing altogether," remarked Rubner.
" It'd take me a long time to explain to you, Mr. Plečka, all
about psychometry, automatism, primary and secondary
indications, and such-like things. But, I tell you, that man
reads a piece of handwriting as if it was a book. And he'll
hit off the one that wrote it as plain as if you saw them in
front of you. He'll tell you what they're like, what their
past record is, what they're thinking about, what they're
keeping back—in fact the whole bag of tricks. I saw him
do it."

" You can't fool me," grunted Mr. Plečka sceptically.

" Well, I'll tell you one particular case," began Mr.
Rubner. " There was a man—I won't tell you his name—
but he's a very well-known man—and he gave Jensen a sheet
of paper with his wife's handwriting. And Jensen just
looked at the writing and began like this : *This woman is
an out-and-out liar, untidy, appallingly sensual and superficial,
lazy, extravagant, always chattering, wants to rule the roost at
home, has got a bad past record, and on top of all that she'd like*

to murder her husband. And, just you imagine, the man went as white as a sheet, because every word of it was true. The funny part of it was that he'd lived happily with her for twenty years and had never noticed a thing. After twenty years of married life with the woman he hadn't discovered a tenth part of what Jensen spotted at the first glance. That wants doing, doesn't it ? Even you must admit there's something in it, Mr. Plečka."

" The only thing that surprises me," observed Mr. Plečka, " is that the fathead of a husband never noticed anything all those twenty years."

" Well, you see," said Mr. Rubner hastily, " the woman was so smart at pretending to be what she wasn't and then the man was quite happy with her. When a man's happy like that he doesn't notice things. And besides, you see, he didn't know about these scientific and exact methods. It's like this : a thing that seems white, when you look at it with the naked eye, is all the colours of the rainbow when science has a go at it. Experience means nothing at all. Nowadays exact methods are the only thing a man can depend upon. So it's no wonder that this particular fellow hadn't the least idea of the monstrosity he was living with. He simply didn't apply scientific methods to her—that's all."

" And I suppose he's going to get a divorce now," suggested Mr. Jančík, the eating-house proprietor.

" I don't know," said Mr. Rubner in casual tones. " I never poke my nose into foolery of that sort. The only thing that interests me about the whole business is how it's possible to discover things from handwriting which otherwise nobody could ever know. Just imagine that for years and years you've had a friend who you thought was a decent, honest chap, and all of a sudden, hey presto ! you discover that he's a thief and a thorough-paced crook. Good Lord,

C

it's no use trusting anyone by their looks. An analysis like that is the only thing that'll show what's inside them."

" Well, I'm blowed ! " exclaimed Mr. Plečka with uneasy surprise. " Why, it's enough to make a man afraid to write to anyone."

" Of course it is," remarked Mr. Rubner. " Just imagine how important this scientific graphology is going to be for tracking down criminals, for instance. Why, they'll be able to lock a man up before he's stolen anything. His handwriting will give him away and show that he's got a secondary bias towards thieving, and, wallop, into quod he goes. There's a tremendous future for that sort of thing. I tell you, it's a regular science, there's not the slightest doubt about it." Mr. Rubner looked at his watch. " Well, it's ten o'clock. Time I was going home."

" Why are you off so early to-day ? " grunted Mr. Plečka.

" Well, you see," said Mr. Rubner gently, " my wife might complain about me leaving her so much by herself."

Proof Positive

"You know, Toník," said Mates, the examining magistrate, to his closest friend, " it's a matter of experience ; I don't believe in any pleas, any alibis or any explanations ; I don't believe the accused or the witnesses. People are liars, even if they don't mean to be ; you get a witness swearing to you that he has no feelings of enmity against the accused and he himself isn't aware that deep down, you know, in his subconscious, he hates him because of some repressed hatred or jealousy. Everything the accused tells you is invented and learnt by rote beforehand ; everything a witness tells you may be the outcome of a conscious or unconscious intention to help or to harm the accused. And by Jove, don't I know it ! People are an utterly dishonest set of brutes.

" Then what are you to believe ? Chance, Toník ; one of those involuntary, unwitting, or—how shall I put it ?— unchecked impulses or actions or words which slip out now and then. Everything can be faked or garbled, everything is sham or is prompted by some ulterior motive, except chance ; you can tell that at the first glance. This is my method : I just sit still and let the people go on babbling whatever they've made up and put into shape beforehand ; I pretend to believe them, in fact I prompt them so as to make them more glib, and then I lie in wait until in spite of themselves they blurt out some tiny word or other that they never intended ; you know, to do that sort of thing properly, you have to be a psychologist. Some examining magistrates make a point of bamboozling the accused ; and so they keep on interrupting him and get him into such a muddle that in

33

the end the silly fool is ready to confess, if necessary, that he murdered the Empress Elizabeth. I want to be absolutely sure of my ground ; that's why I wait steadily, patiently, until this systematic lying and pretending that among experts is known as a confession inadvertently produces a flash of truth. You know, in this vale of tears, you can only get at the pure truth as the result of an oversight, when a human being makes a slip of the tongue or does something by mistake.

" Look here, Toník, I've got no secrets from you ; we've been friends ever since we were boys—you remember how they gave you a good hiding when I broke a window. I wouldn't tell anyone about it, but there's something I'm so ashamed of that I've got to get it off my mind ; it's no use, a man can't do without confession. I'll tell you how well that method of mine worked just recently in my—in my most private life ; in fact, in my marriage. And then you can tell me, if you feel like it, that I was a fool and a cad ; I deserve it.

" Well, old fellow, I—yes, I suspected my wife, Martha ; in fact I was frantically jealous. I got it into my head that she was carrying on with that—with young what's-his-name —I'll call him Arthur ; I don't think you know him. Of course, I'm not a cad ; if I knew for certain that she loved him, I'd say : Martha, you go your way and I'll go mine. But the worst of it was, I didn't know for certain ; Toník, you haven't any idea what a torment that can be. By Jove ! I had a horrible year of it. You know the kind of monkey-tricks a jealous husband will get up to : he shadows his wife, he watches her, he cross-questions the servants, he causes scenes. But you must bear in mind, too, that I happen to be an examining magistrate ; my dear fellow, my domestic life for the past year has been one continual cross-examination from morning till—till bedtime.

" The accused, I mean, Martha, stood her ground splendidly ; whether she cried, whether she was offended and wouldn't say a word, whether she gave a full account of where she'd been all day and what she'd been doing, it was a waste of time for me to try to detect her making a slip of the tongue or otherwise giving herself away. Of course, she often used to lie to me, I mean, she used to lie as a matter of course, but that's just a woman's way ; a woman will never tell you straightforwardly that she was two hours at the dressmaker's—she'll make out that she was at the dentist's or in the cemetery at her mother's grave. The more I worried her—Tonda, a fellow who's jealous is worse than a mad dog—the more I bullied her, the less sure I was of my ground. Every word she uttered, every excuse she made, I brooded over them, I took stock of them, but I discovered nothing but the usual deliberate half-truths and half-lies that make up normal human relationships and marriage in particular, don't they ? I know how it made me feel ; but when I consider what poor Martha must have gone through, well, my dear fellow, I could just about kick myself.

" Now this year Martha went off to Franzensbad—you know, these women's ailments, and so on, as a matter of fact she wasn't looking at all well. Needless to say, I had her watched there—I paid a shabby fellow to do the job, and incidentally he just loafed about from one pub to another. It's a funny thing how your whole life goes wrong when there's only one single detail of it that isn't what it should be ; if you've got a stain in a single spot, you feel dirty all over. Martha wrote to me in a sort of uncertain and subdued way as if she couldn't make out what was the matter ; of course I probed into her letters and searched between the lines. And then one day I got a letter from her, addressed : František Mates, examining magistrate and so forth ; and when I opened the envelope and took out the sheet of note-paper, the first thing I saw was : ' Dear Arthur.'

" My word, how my hands shook. So at last here it was. It does occasionally happen when you've been writing several letters that you put some of them into the wrong envelopes. A silly trick for chance to play Martha, wasn't it ? That's what I thought, until, my dear chap, I felt sorry for her that she'd given herself away like that.

" Don't misunderstand me, Toník, my first impulse was not to read the letter intended for this—this Arthur, but to send it back to Martha ; I'd have done that anyhow, but jealousy is an ugly business and makes you do mean things ; well, old fellow, I read that letter and I'll show it to you, because I carry it about with me. Just have a look at it.

" ' Dear Arthur,
' Please don't be angry with me for not having answered your letter before this ; but I've been so worried because Franci—that's me, of course—hadn't written for such a long time ; I know he's frightfully busy, but after being so long without any news about my husband, I was going about like a lost soul ; but, of course, you wouldn't understand that. Franci's coming here next month, so perhaps you could come too. He writes to say that he's got a most interesting case on at present ; he doesn't say what it is, but I think it's the murder Hugo Muller committed ; I should be frightfully interested to hear about it. I'm sorry that you and Franci haven't been seeing much of each other lately, but that's only because he's so frightfully busy ; if things had been as before, you might have got him to be more sociable or to go on a motor-trip. You always used to be so nice to us and even now you haven't forgotten us, although things aren't as they should be ; Franci is so nervous and queer. You haven't told me how your sweetheart is.

Franci complains that it's frightfully hot in Prague ; he ought to come here and take things easy, but I'm sure he's working in his office till late at night. When are you going to the seaside ? I hope you're taking your sweetheart with you ; you've got no idea what it means for us women to long for anyone.

With best wishes,

Yours very sincerely,

MARTHA MATESOVA.'

" Well, Toník, what do you think of that ? I know it's not a very witty letter ; it's quite a feeble effort as regards style and interest ; but, my dear fellow, what a light it throws on Martha and her attitude towards that wretched Arthur ! I'd never have believed her if she'd told me what she wanted ; but here I'd got hold of something quite inadvertently, quite beyond her will. So you see that the truth, pure and simple, is revealed only as the result of an oversight. I could have howled for joy—and also shame, at having been so stupidly jealous.

" What did I do then ? Why, I tied some string round the papers concerning the Hugo Muller murder, locked them up in a drawer, and the next day I was in Franzensbad. When Martha saw me she turned red and stammered like a little girl ; anyone would have thought that she had done something outrageous. I kept a straight face. ' Franci,' said Martha presently, ' did you get my letter ? '

" ' What letter ? ' I said in a tone of surprise. ' You write to me confoundedly seldom.'

" Martha looked at me in a startled kind of way and sighed as if a load had been taken off her mind. ' Why, then I must have forgotten to post it to you,' she said, and fumbled in her bag where she fished out a rather crumpled letter. It began : Dear Franci : I couldn't help laughing

to myself.   I suppose that Mr. Arthur must have sent back
by return of post the letter that wasn't meant for him.

" Then not another word was said about the whole
business.   Of course, I began to tell her about Hugo Muller's
crime, which interested her so much.   I believe that to this
very day she believes I never received that letter.

" Well, that's the whole story ; ever since then there's
been at least peace in our household.   I say, wasn't I a fool
to be so beastly jealous ?   You know, now I'm trying to
make amends to Martha for it ; it wasn't till I read her
letter that I realized how much the poor thing worries about
me.   Well, now it's off my mind ; a man's more ashamed
when he's made a fool of himself than when he's committed
a sin.

" But there's a typical example for you of how a thing can
be proved beyond the shadow of a doubt by sheer downright
chance, isn't it ? "

Somewhere about the same time, the young man, here
known as Arthur, said to Martha : " Well, pet, did it work?"

" What, darling ? "

" The letter you sent him that time by mistake."

" I should think it did," said Martha, and lapsed into
thought ; " you know, dear, it makes me feel quite ashamed
how awfully much he believes me now.   Ever since then
he's been so nice to me.   Just fancy, he carries that letter
about with him next to his heart."   Martha trembled
slightly.   " It's really frightful the way I'm—I'm deceiving
him, don't you think so ? "

But Mr. Arthur didn't think so ; at least he said that most
decidedly he didn't.

The Fortune-Teller

★ ★ ★

EVERYBODY WHO knows anything about the subject will realize that this episode could not have happened in Czechoslovakia, or in France, or in Germany, for in all these countries, as you are aware, judges•are bound to try offenders and to sentence them in accordance with the letter of the law and not in accordance with their shrewd common-sense and the dictates of their consciences. And the fact that in this story there is a judge who, in passing sentence, was guided not by the statute-book, but by sound common-sense, is due to the circumstance that the incident which I am about to relate could have happened nowhere else than in England ; in fact, it happened in London, or to be more precise, in Kensington ; no, wait a bit, it was in Brompton or Bayswater—anyway somewhere thereabouts. The judge was, as a matter of fact, a magistrate, and his name was Mr. Kelly, J.P. Also there was a lady, and her name was plain Myers. Mrs. Edith Myers.

Well, I must tell you that this lady, who was otherwise a respectable person, came under the notice of Detective-Inspector MacLeary.

" My dear," said MacLeary to his wife one evening, " I can't get that Mrs. Myers out of my head. What I'd like to know is, how the woman makes her living. Just fancy, here we are in the month of February and she's sent her servant for asparagus. And I've discovered that she has between twelve and twenty visitors every day, and they vary from charwomen to duchesses. I know, darling, you'll say she's probably a fortune-teller. Very likely, but that can only be a blind for something else, say, the white slave traffic or espionage. Look here, I'd rather like to get to the bottom of it."

" All right, Bob," said the excellent Mrs. MacLeary, " you leave it to me."

And so it came about that on the following day, Mrs. MacLeary, of course without her wedding ring, but on the other hand very girlishly dressed and with her hair in ringlets like a young woman who feels that it is time for her to put away frivolities, with a scared look on her baby face, rang at Mrs. Myers's door in Bayswater or possibly Marylebone. She had to wait quite a while before Mrs. Myers received her.

" Sit down, my dear," said the old lady, when she had very thoroughly inspected her shy visitor. " What can I do for you ? "

" I—I—I—— " stammered Mrs. MacLeary. " I'd like —it's my twentieth birthday to-morrow—I'm awfully anxious to know about my future."

" But, Miss—er, what name, please ? " quoth Mrs. Myers, and seized a pack of cards which she began to shuffle energetically.

" Jones," sighed Mrs. MacLeary.

" My dear Miss Jones," continued Mrs. Myers, " don't misunderstand me. I don't tell fortunes by cards, except, of course, just now and then, to oblige a friend, as every old woman does. Take the cards in your left hand and divide them into five heaps. That's right. Sometimes I read the cards as a pastime, but apart from that—dear me ! " she said, cutting the first heap. " Diamonds ! That means money. And the knave of hearts. That's a nice hand."

"Ah," said Mrs. MacLeary, " and what else? "

" Knave of diamonds," proceeded Mrs. Myers, uncovering the second heap. " Ten of spades, that's a journey. But here ! " she exclaimed. " I see clubs. Clubs always mean worry, but there's a queen of hearts at the bottom."

" What does that mean ? " asked Mrs. MacLeary, opening her eyes as wide as she could.

" Diamonds again," meditated Mrs. Myers over the third heap. " My dear, there's lots of money in store for you ; but I can't tell yet whether you're going on a long journey or whether it's someone near and dear to you."

" I've got to go to Southampton to see my aunt," remarked Mrs. MacLeary.

" That must be the long journey," said Mrs. Myers, cutting the fourth heap. " Somebody's going to get in your way, some elderly man——"

" I expect that's my uncle ! " exclaimed Mrs. MacLeary.

" Well, here we've got something and no mistake," declared Mrs. Myers over the fifth heap. " My dear Miss Jones, this is the nicest hand I've ever seen. There'll be a wedding before the year's out ; a very, very rich young man is going to marry you—he must be a millionaire or a business man, because he travels a lot ; but before you are united, you'll have to overcome great obstacles; there's an elderly gentleman who'll get in your way, but you must persevere. When you do get married you'll move a long way off, most likely across the ocean. My fee's a guinea, for the Christian mission to the poor negroes."

" I'm so grateful to you," declared Mrs. MacLeary, taking one pound and one shilling out of her handbag, " awfully grateful. Mrs. Myers, what would it cost without any of those worries ? "

" The cards can't be bribed," said the old lady with dignity. " What is your uncle ? "

" He's in the police," lied the young lady with an innocent face. " You know, the secret service."

" Oh ! " said the old lady, and drew three cards out of the heap. " That's very nasty, very nasty. Tell him, my dear, that he's threatened by a great danger. He ought to come and see me, to find out more about it. There's lots of them from Scotland Yard come here and get me to read the cards for them, and they all tell me what they have on their minds. Yes, just you send him to me. You say he's on secret service work ? Mr. Jones ? Tell him I'll be expecting him. Good-bye, dear Miss Jones. Next, please ! "

" I don't like the look of this," said Mr. MacLeary, scratching his neck reflectively. " I don't like the look of this, Katie. That woman was too much interested in your late uncle. Besides that, her real name isn't Myers, but Meierhofer, and she hails from Lübeck. A damned German ! " growled Mr. MacLeary. " I wonder how we can stop her little game ? I wouldn't mind betting five to one that she worms things out of people that are no business of hers. I'll tell you what ; I'll pass the word on to the bosses."

And Mr. MacLeary did, in good sooth, pass the word on to the bosses. Oddly enough, the bosses took a serious view of the matter, and so it came about that the worthy Mrs. Myers was summoned to appear before Mr. Kelly, J.P.

" Well, Mrs. Myers," the magistrate said to her, " what's all this I hear about this fortune-telling of yours with cards?"

" Good gracious, your worship," said the old lady, " I must do something for a living. At my age I can't go on the music-halls and dance ! "

" Hm," said Mr. Kelly. " But the charge against you is that you don't read the cards properly. My dear good lady, that's as bad as if you were to give people slabs of clay when they ask for cakes of chocolate. In return for a fee of one guinea people are entitled to a correct prophecy. Look here now, what's the good of your trying to prophesy when you don't know how to ? "

" It isn't everyone who complains," urged the old lady in her defence. " You see, I foretell the things they like. The pleasure they get out of it is worth a few shillings, your worship. And sometimes I'm right. *Mrs. Myers*, said one lady to me, *nobody's ever read the cards for me as well as you have and given me such good advice.* She lives in St. John's Wood and is getting a divorce from her husband."

" Look here," the magistrate cut her short. " We've got a witness against you. Mrs. MacLeary, tell the court what happened."

" Mrs. Myers told me from the cards," began Mrs. Mac-Leary glibly, " that before the year was out I'd be married, that my future husband would be a rich young man and that I'd go with him across the ocean——'

" Why across the ocean particularly ? " inquired the magistrate.

" Because there was the nine of spades in the second heap ; Mrs. Myers said that means journeys."

" Rubbish ! " growled the magistrate. " The nine of spades means hope. It's the jack of spades that means journeys ; and when it turns up with the seven of diamonds, that means long journeys that are likely to lead to something worth while. Mrs. Myers, you can't bamboozle me. You prophesied to the witness here that before the year was out she'd marry a rich young man. But Mrs. MacLeary has been married for the last three years to Detective-Inspector MacLeary, and a fine fellow he is too. Mrs. Myers, how do you explain that absurdity ? "

" My goodness me ! " said the old lady placidly. " That does happen now and then. When this young person called on me she was all dressed up, but her left glove was torn. So that looked as if she wasn't too well off, but she wanted to make a good impression. Then she said she was twenty, but now it turns out she's twenty-five——"

" Twenty-four," Mrs. MacLeary burst forth.

" That's all the same. Well, she wanted to get married,

what I mean to say, she made out to me she wasn't married. So I arranged a set of cards for her that'd mean a wedding and a rich husband. I thought that'd meet the case better than anything else."

"And what about the obstacles, the elderly gentleman and the journey across the ocean ? " asked Mrs. MacLeary.

"That was to give you plenty for your money," said Mrs. Myers artlessly. "There's quite a lot has to be told for a guinea."

"Well, that's enough," said the magistrate. "Mrs. Myers, it's no use. The way you tell fortunes by cards is a fraud. Cards take some understanding. Of course, there are various ideas about it, but, if my memory serves me, the nine of spades never means journeys. You'll pay a fine of fifty pounds, just the same as people who adulterate food or sell worthless goods. There's a suspicion, too, Mrs. Myers, that you're engaged in espionage as well. But I don't expect you'll admit that."

"As true as I'm standing here——" exclaimed Mrs. Myers.

But Mr. Kelly interrupted her. "Well, we'll say no more about that. But as you're an alien without any proper means of subsistence, the authorities will make use of the powers vested in them and will have you deported. Goodbye, Mrs. Myers, and thank you, Mrs. MacLeary. I must say that this inaccurate fortune-telling is a disgraceful and unscrupulous business. Just bear that in mind, Mrs. Myers."

"What am I to do now ? " sighed the old lady. "Just when I was beginning to get a good connexion together——"

About a year later Mr. Kelly met Detective-Inspector MacLeary.

"Fine weather," said the magistrate amiably. "By the way, how is Mrs. MacLeary ? "

Mr. MacLeary looked very glum. "Well—you know, Mr.

Kelly," he said with a certain embarrassment, " Mrs. Mac-Leary—well, the fact is—she's left me."

" You don't say so," said the magistrate in astonishment, " such a nice young lady, too ! "

" That's just it," growled Mr. MacLeary. " Some young whipper-snapper went crazy about her before I knew what was happening. He's a millionaire, or a business-man from Melbourne. I tried to stop her, but——" Mr. MacLeary made a helpless gesture with his hand, " a week ago they sailed together for Australia."

There was Something Shady about the Man

★   ★   ★

"MR. KOLDA," said Mr. Pacovský to Sergeant Kolda, "I've got something for you." It should be explained that under Austria Mr. Pacovský had been in the police, a mounted policeman in fact, but after the war he somehow didn't fit in with the new conditions, retired, did a bit of foreign travel and then became the landlord of the Prospect Inn. The place is a bit lonely, but nowadays it's beginning to get popular, what with the excursions, the views, the bathing in the pond and such-like attractions.

"Mr. Kolda," said Mr. Pacovský, "there's something about this I can't make out. I've got a fellow staying at my place ; he's been there for the past fortnight. His name's Roedl. What it is I don't know ; he pays his way, he don't drink and he don't gamble, but—I'll tell you what," said Mr. Pacovský suddenly, "come over and have a look at him some time."

"What's wrong with him ? " asked Mr. Kolda.

"That's just it," said Mr. Pacovský in a tone of annoyance. "I don't know. There's nothing you can exactly point to and yet—how shall I put it ?—there's something shady about him to my mind. There you've got it."

"Roedl, Roedl, reflected Sergeant Kolda. "The name don't suggest anything to me. What is he ? "

"I don't know," said Mr. Pacovský. "He says he's a bank clerk ; but I can't get out of him what bank he works at. I don't like the look of it. He's a polite enough chap, but—— And he never gets any letters, either. It looks

46

to me as if he was keeping out of people's way. And I don't like the look of it."

" How do you mean—" inquired Sergeant Kolda, " keeping out of people's way ? "

" He don't exactly keep out of their way," said Mr. Pacovský nonplussed, " but—hang it all, who wants to stay in the country in September ? And whenever a car stops in front of the place he goes straight to his room, even if he's in the middle of a meal. I tell you, there's something shady about this chap Roedl."

Mr. Kolda meditated for a while. " Well, I'll tell you what, Mr. Pacovský," he remarked with a sage air ; "supposing you was to tell him you're going to shut the place up for the autumn. He can go to Prague or to some other locality, can't he ? Why should we, more than anyone else, have him on our hands ? And there you are."

The next day, a Sunday, Hurych, a young policeman, whose nickname was Mary Ann or Girlie, was going off duty ; on the way it occurred to him that he might call at the inn, and he made straight from the woods to the yard of the Prospect Inn. When he had reached the back entrance, he stopped to blow the ashes out of his pipe. At that instant he heard the rattle of a window on the first floor looking on to the yard, and something bumped on the ground behind him. Girlie ran into the yard and caught hold of a man who for no reason at all had just jumped out of the window.

" Look here," he said disapprovingly, " what are you up to ? "

The man he was holding by the shoulder looked pale and expressionless. " Why shouldn't I jump ? " he remarked feebly. " This is where I live."

P.C. Girlie reflected briefly on the situation. " Maybe you do," he said, " but I don't like you jumping out of the window."

D

" I didn't know it wasn't allowed," the expressionless man excused himself. " Ask Mr. Pacovský whether I live here. My name's Roedl."

" May be it is," said P.C. Girlie. " Then show me your papers."

" Papers," said Mr. Roedl hesitantly. " I haven't got any papers with me. I'll write for them."

" We'll write for them ourselves," said Girlie readily. ' You come along with me, Mr. Roedl."

" Where to ? " objected Mr. Roedl, as white as a sheet. " What business—what business have you got to run me in ? "

" Because there's something shady about you, Mr. Roedl," declared Girlie. " Just you hold your tongue and come along with me."

At the police-station Sergeant Kolda was sitting in his slippers, smoking a long pipe and reading the official police bulletin. When he saw Girlie with Mr. Roedl, he kicked up a row : " Why, hang it all, Mary Ann, what do you think you're up to ? Can't I have a bit of peace even on a Sunday? What do you want to bring people here for on a Sunday of all days ? "

" Well, sergeant," declared Girlie, " there's something shady about this man. When he saw me going to the inn he jumped out of the window into the yard and tried to slip away into the woods. And he hasn't got any papers. So I ran him in. His name's Roedl."

" Aha ! " said Mr. Kolda with interest, " Mr. Roedl. So now we've got you, Mr. Roedl ! "

" But you can't arrest me," said Mr. Roedl in a disgruntled tone.

" No, we can't," agreed Mr. Kolda. " But we can keep you here, can't we ? Mary Ann, just step across to the inn, search Mr. Roedl's room and have his things brought here. Sit down, Mr. Roedl."

" I—I decline to make any statement," stammered Mr. Roedl with signs of agitation. " I'll complain—I protest—"

" Now then, Mr. Roedl," sighed Mr. Kolda, " there's something shady about you. I'm not going to argue the point with you. Sit down there and shut up."

Whereupon he picked up his paper and went on reading.

" Look here, Mr. Roedl," he said presently, " anybody can see by the look of you that there's something wrong with you. If I was you I'd own up and then your mind'll be at rest. But if you don't want to, well and good."

Mr. Roedl sat there pale and bathed in sweat. Mr. Kolda watched him, snorting with disgust, and then he went to turn over the mushrooms which he was frying on the stove.

" Now just you listen to me, Mr. Roedl," he resumed after an interval, " we're going to fix your identity ; and you'll be kept in custody the while and you'll have nobody to talk to. My dear sir, don't make yourself a nuisance ! "

Mr. Roedl continued in his dogged silence and Mr. Kolda, growling with annoyance, cleaned his pipe. " Yes," he said, " and let me tell you this much : it may take us a month to find out who you are, but that month, Mr. Roedl, won't be reckoned as part of your sentence. It'd be a pity, I must say, to lose a month of your sentence like that."

" And if I own up," said Mr. Roedl wavering, " then——"

" Then you'll be remanded in custody, see," explained Mr. Kolda, " and that'll be reckoned in. Do just whatever you like. There's something shady about you and I'll be glad when they take you off to the assizes. So now you know, Mr. Roedl."

Mr. Roedl sighed ; his shifty eyes had a woe-begone and almost cowed expression in them. " Why—" he blurted out, " why does everyone say that there's something shady about me ? "

" Because you look scared," quoth Mr. Kolda sturdily. " You're hiding something, Mr. Roedl, and people don't like that. Why don't you look anyone straight in the face ? You're uneasy. That's what it is, Mr. Roedl."

" Rosner," said the pale-faced man by way of correction.

Mr. Kolda pondered. " Rosner, Rosner, let's see now, which Rosner ? The name sounds familiar to me somehow."

" Why Ferdinand Rosner, of course," the man blurted out.

" Ferdinand Rosner," repeated Mr. Kolda, " now I'm getting at it. Ferdinand Rosner——"

" The Vienna Deposit Bank," prompted the pale-faced man.

" Aha ! " exclaimed Mr. Kolda joyfully. " Embezzlement ! Now I've got it. Why, of course, Rosner ! My good man, we've had a warrant against you for the last three years. So you're Rosner," he repeated in accents of delight. " Why on earth didn't you say so at once. Just fancy, here was I nearly kicking you out and you're Rosner ! Mary Ann," he bawled gleefully at the constable Hurych who was just coming in, " this is Rosner, who's wanted for fraud."

" That is——" Rosner winced slightly.

" Come, come, Rosner," said Mr. Kolda soothingly, " you'll get used to that. Think yourself lucky you've got it off your chest at last. But, my good man, for Heaven's sake, where have you been lying low for the last three years?"

" Lying low," said Rosner bitterly. " Either in sleeping-cars or in swell hotels. They don't ask you who you are and where you come from."

" Dear me," said Mr. Kolda sympathetically, " that must have cost you the deuce of a lot, eh ? "

" I should say so," said Rosner with a sigh of relief. " But I couldn't very well go to the sort of place that's always being raided by the cops, could I ?   No, sir, I had to keep living above my means.   I never stayed anywhere for more than three nights, till I came here—and now you've collared me."

" Why, yes," said Mr. Kolda in comforting tones, " but your money was running short, wasn't it ?   And then the game would have been up anyway."

" Yes," agreed Rosner.   " But I tell you, I couldn't have stood it much longer.   Good Lord, for the last three years I've never had a good heart-to-heart talk with anyone, till now.   Why, I couldn't even have a square meal.   As soon as anyone took a look at me I had to make myself scarce. And everyone used to take stock of me," complained Mr. Rosner.   " I used to fancy that everyone was from the police.   Just imagine, even Mr. Pacovský."

" Don't worry yourself about that," said Mr. Kolda. " You see, Mr. Pacovský used to be in the police."

" There you are," growled Rosner, " and then you expect the likes of me to escape notice.   Why does everyone take stock of me like that ?   Do I look like a criminal ? "

Mr. Kolda scanned him attentively.   " I'll tell you what, Rosner," he said, " not now you don't ; now you look just like any other man.   But before, there was something shady about you, my lad.   I don't know why it was that you struck me as sort of queer.   Well, anyway," he decided, " Mary Ann's going to take you to the cells.   It ain't six o'clock yet, so we'll reckon to-day as part of your sentence. If it wasn't Sunday, I'd take you there myself, just to show that, hm, that there's no ill-feeling.   It was only because you seemed a bit odd, Rosner, but that's all right now. Mary Ann, take him to the lock-up."

" You know, Mary Ann," said Mr. Kolda that evening, " I don't mind telling you I quite liked that chap Rosner. A thoroughly decent sort of fellow, ain't he ? I don't suppose he'll get more than a year."

" I put a good word in for him," said P.C. Girlie, blushing, " and asked them to let him have two blankets. He ain't used to sleeping on a truckle-bed."

" That's right," observed Mr. Kolda. " And I'll tell the warder to have a talk to him now and then. Just so as this chap Rosner can see he's among friends again."

The Strange Experiences of Mr. Janik

★ ★ ★

THIS MR. JANIK is neither Dr. Janik who is in one of the Ministries, nor the Janik who shot the estate-owner Jirsa, nor the stockbroker Janik who is said to have made a break of 326 at billiards, but Mr. Janik, the head of the firm of Janik & Holeček, wholesale dealers in paper and cellulose. He is a shortish, gentlemanly person who once courted Miss Severová and was so upset when she refused him that he never married ; he is, in fact, to avoid all possibility of a misunderstanding, the Janik known as Janik, the stationer.

Now this Mr. Janik got mixed up in these matters by sheer chance. It started at some place on the Sázava where he was spending his summer holidays. That was when they were searching for the corpse of Růžena Regnerová who was murdered by her fiancé Jindřich Bašta. He soaked the poor creature in paraffin oil, burnt her and buried the body in a forest. Although Bašta was found guilty of having murdered Růžena, no trace of her body or her bones could be found. For nine days the gendarmes had been tramping about in the forests under the guidance of Bašta, who kept telling them the place : it was here or it was there ; they burrowed and dug but nothing could they find. It was clear that Bašta in his desperation was leading them astray or was trying to gain time. This Jindřich Bašta was a young man of a respectable and well-to-do family, but likely enough the doctor had somehow squeezed his head with the forceps before he had arrived into the world. At any rate there was something wrong with him ; he was a queer,

degenerate sort of fellow.   For nine days he had been leading
the gendarmes about in the woods, as pale as a ghost, his
eyes twitching with a nystagmus of horror—he was a dis-
tressing sight.   The gendarmes trudged with him through
bilberries and swamps ;   they were now so savage that it
would not have taken much to make them let fly, and they
were thinking to themselves, you brute, we'll give you such
a rough time of it that you'll take us to the right place in the
end.   Bašta, who was so worn out that he could scarcely
drag himself along, sank down on the ground at random and
gasped :   " This is where I buried her ! "

" Get up, Bašta," a gendarme bellowed at him.   " It
wasn't here.   On you go ! "

Bašta stood up totteringly and staggered on a little
farther until he again collapsed with exhaustion.   The procession was something after this style : four gendarmes, one
or two gamekeepers and some old fellows with shovels, and
Jindřich Bašta, a livid wreck of a man, convulsively shuffling
along.

Mr. Janik knew the gendarmes from the local inn ;
accordingly he was allowed to join this tragic procession
through the woods, without being churlishly told to clear
off.   Moreover, he was carrying with him some tins of
sardines, salami, cognac, and suchlike commodities, which
came in very handy.   On the ninth day things were bad, so
bad that Mr. Janik had made up his mind : no more of this
for me.   The gendarmes were fairly growling with sullen
rage, the gamekeepers were saying that they'd had enough
of it and that they'd got other things to do, the old fellows
with the shovels were grumbling that 20 crowns a day
wasn't much for a tough job like that, and crumpled up on
the ground, Jindřich was shaking in convulsive fits, no
longer replying to the shouts and bullying of the gendarmes.
At this dreary and bewildering moment Mr. Janik did some-

thing which, so to speak, was not on the programme : he kneeled down beside Bašta, thrust a ham-roll into his hand and said pityingly : " Look here, Mr. Bašta, come, come now, Mr. Bašta, this won't do, you know." Bašta uttered a wail and burst out crying. " I'll find it . . . I'll find it, you'll see," he sobbed, and tried to stand up ; whereupon one of the plain-clothes men came up and lifted him to his feet almost tenderly. " Just you lean on me, Mr. Bašta," he coaxed him. " Mr. Janik'll take hold of you from the other side ; that's it. Now then, Mr. Bašta, you'll show Mr. Janik where it was, won't you ? "

An hour later, Jindřich Bašta, smoking a cigarette, stood above a shallow pit from which a thigh-bone was sticking up.

" Is that the body of Růžena Regnerová ? " asked Sergeant Trunka grimly.

" Yes," said Jindřich Bašta calmly, and flicked some cigarette-ash into the open pit. " Is there anything else you want ? "

" You know, sir," Sergeant Trunka held forth to Mr. Janik that evening in the local inn. " You do know how to get round people; and no mistake. Well, here's my best respects, sir. That chap threw up the sponge as soon as you said ' Mr. Bašta ' to him. Well, he kept it up long enough, goodness knows, the brute. But if you don't mind me asking, sir, how did you know that being polite to him was going to have an effect like that ? "

" Oh," said the hero of the day, with a modest blush, " that was only by the way, you know. I say ' sir ' to everyone. And then I felt sorry for him and so I thought I'd offer him that roll——"

" That's instinct," announced Sergeant Trunka. " That's what I call having a flair for things. Here's my best respects, Mr. Janik. You ought to join the force. We could do with a man like you."

Some time after that Mr. Janik was travelling by the night-train to Bratislava : some Slovak paper-factory had arranged its general meeting of shareholders there, and as Mr. Janik had a tidy sum invested in it he was anxious to attend. " Wake me up before we get to Bratislava," he said to the guard, " or else I'll get taken as far as the frontier." Whereupon he crawled into his bed in the sleeping-car, glad of having a compartment to himself, made himself thoroughly cosy, meditated for a while on various business matters and then fell asleep. Nor was he aware what time it was when the guard opened the door of the compartment for a passenger who began to undress and clambered into the top bunk. In a half-dream Mr. Janik saw a pair of pants and two extraordinarily hairy legs dangling down, heard the grunting of someone who was wrapping himself up in the bed-covers, then there was a click of the switch and clattering darkness again. Mr. Janik dreamt a number of things, mostly that he was being pursued by some hairy legs, and then he was woken up by a long stillness and the sound of somebody outside who was saying : " See you again at Žilina." He jumped out of bed and looked through the window ; he saw that day was breaking, that the train was in the station at Bratislava and that the guard had forgotten to wake him up. He was so scared that he forgot to curse, and with feverish rapidity he dragged his trousers and the rest of his clothes over his pyjamas, shoved all his odds and ends into his pockets and jumped on to the platform just as the guard was giving the signal for the train to start.

" Whew ! " gasped Mr. Janik, shook his fist at the departing express, and went to the lavatory to finish dressing. When he had sorted out the contents of his pockets he was flabbergasted ; in his breast-pocket, instead of one note-case, he had two. The fatter of the two, which was not his, contained sixty new Czechoslovak notes of five hundred crowns each. This evidently belonged to his fellow-passenger of the previous night ; but how it had got into his pocket Mr. Janik, still half asleep, couldn't for the life of him imagine. All right, of course the first thing to do was to get hold of someone from the police to whom he could hand over the stranger's note-case. The police left Mr. Janik for a while on the verge of starvation, and in the meantime telephoned to Galanta, telling the people there to inform the traveller in sleeping-berth No. 14 that his note-case with contents was at the police-station in Bratislava. Then Mr. Janik had to give particulars about himself, whereupon he went and got some breakfast. Then someone from the police looked him up and asked him whether there wasn't a mistake ; for it appeared that the gentleman in sleeping-berth No. 14 had denied having lost any note-case. Mr. Janik had to go back to the police-station and explain once more how the note-case came into his possession. Meanwhile two plain-clothes men had taken the sixty bank-notes away with them and Mr. Janik had to wait half an hour between two detectives, after which he was led before some bigwig of the police.

" Look here," said the bigwig. " We're just sending a wire to Parkán-Nána to detain that man in sleeping-berth No. 14. Can you give us an exact description of him ? "

Practically all that Mr. Janik could say was that the traveller had remarkably hairy legs. The bigwig was not oversatisfied with this. " You see, those bank-notes are forgeries," he said suddenly. " You'll have to stay here until we confront you with your fellow-traveller."

Quite privately Mr. Janik cursed the guard who had not woken him in time and who had thus caused Mr. Janik in his flurry to get that confounded note-case into his pocket. After about an hour a telegram arrived from Parkán-Nána, to the effect that the traveller in sleeping-berth No. 14 had left the train at Nové Zámky ; where he had gone to, either on foot or otherwise, after that, was so far unknown.

" Well, Mr. Janik," said the bigwig at last, " we won't keep you here any longer just now ; we're turning this matter over to Inspector Hrušek in Prague for him to look into these forgeries. But if you ask me, it's a very serious business. Now you get back to Prague as soon as you can and the people there'll send for-you. In the meantime I'd like to thank you for having collared those forged notes so neatly. You can't tell me that's only a lucky chance."

Scarcely had Mr. Janik returned to Prague than he was sent for by the authorities at police-headquarters ; there he was received by a huge, thick-set gentleman who was addressed by everyone as " President," and a sallow and scraggy person whose name was Inspector Hruška.

" Sit down, Mr. Janik," said the thick-set gentleman, as he broke the seals on a small packet. " Is this the note-case that you—er—that you found in your pocket at Bratislava?"

" Yes," sighed Mr. Janik.

The thick-set gentleman counted over the new bank-notes which were in the pocket-book. " Sixty of them," he said. " All belonging to series 27,451. That was the figure that had already been reported to us from Cheb."

The scraggy man picked up one of the bank-notes, closed his eyes and rubbed it between his fingers, after which he sniffed at it. " These here must be from Graz," he said. " The ones from Geneva are not so sticky."

" Graz," repeated the thick-set gentleman meditatively. " That's where they make these things for Budapest, isn't it ? "

The scraggy man merely blinked. " Supposing I went to Vienna," he suggested, " but the police at Vienna won't hand the fellow over."

" Hm," grunted the thick-set gentleman. " Then find out

some other way for us to get hold of him. If the worst comes to the worst, tell them we'll exchange him for Leberhardt. Well, a pleasant journey, Hruška. And now, sir," he said, turning to Mr. Janik, " I really don't know how I'm to thank you. You're the one who discovered where Jindřich Bašta's girl was, aren't you ? "

Mr. Janik turned red. " That was only a fluke," he said hastily. " I really—I never meant to——"

" You've got a flair for things, Mr. Janik," quoth the thick-set gentleman approvingly. " And it's a rare gift. There are people who for the life of them can't discover anything, while others just hit on the very finest clues. You ought to join us, Mr. Janik."

" I'm afraid I can't," parried Mr. Janik. " I—you see, I've got a business of my own—doing well—an old-established firm that used to belong to my grandfather——"

" Please yourself," sighed the great man, " but it's a pity all the same. It isn't everyone who's got such confounded good luck as you have. I hope we meet again, Mr. Janik."

About a month after that, Mr. Janik was having supper with a business friend from Leipzig. As a matter of course, at a supper of that kind, between business men, things are done in style ; the cognac in particular was quite exceptionally good ; and the end of it was, that Mr. Janik declined point-blank to proceed home on foot. He beckoned to the waiter and commanded a taxi.

On leaving the hotel he saw a taxi waiting in front of the entrance ; so he got inside, slammed the door, and in his gleefulness clean forgot that he had not told the chauffeur where he lived. Nevertheless, the taxi started off, and Mr. Janik, comfortably ensconced in a corner, fell asleep.

He had no idea how long the drive lasted ; but he was woken up by the stopping of the taxi, and the chauffeur opened the door for him, saying : " Here we are, sir. You're to go upstairs, sir." Mr. Janik wondered very much where he could be; but as he didn't care what happened after all the cognac he'd drunk he went up some stairs and opened a door, behind which he heard a noisy conversation. There were about twenty men in the room, and as he entered they looked eagerly towards the door. Suddenly there was a strange stillness ; one of the men stood up and came towards Mr. Janik, demanding : " What do you want here ? Who are you ? "

Mr. Janik gazed around him in surprise ; he recognized five or six of those present—they were well-to-do persons who, it was rumoured, had a political axe to grind ; but Mr. Janik never meddled in politics. " Good Lord," he said affably, " why, fancy seeing Mr. Koubek and Mr. Heller here. Cheerio, Ferry, I could do with a drink."

" How did this chap get here ? " snarled one of the company. " Is he one of us ? "

Two individuals pushed Mr. Janik into the passage. " How did you get here ? " asked one of them gruffly. " Who asked you to come here ? "

Mr. Janik was sobered by this lack of friendliness. " Where am I ? " he inquired indignantly. " Where the devil have you brought me to ? "

One of the two individuals ran downstairs and pounced upon the chauffeur. " You damned fool ! " he yelled. " Where did you pick this chap up ? "

" Why, in front of the hotel," replied the chauffeur, on the defensive. " I was told this afternoon that at ten o'clock this evening I was to wait by the hotel for a gentleman and bring him here. This here gentleman got into my cab at ten o'clock and never said a word to me ; so I just brought him straight along——"

" Good God ! " shouted the individual below. " It's the

wrong man. You've got us into a fine mess, and no mistake."

Mr. Janik sat down resignedly on the stairs. " Aha," he said complacently, " a secret meeting, eh ? Now you'll have to strangle me and bury the corpse. Let's have a glass of water."

" Look here," said one of the two men. " You've made a mistake. That wasn't Mr. Koubek or Mr. Heller inside there, see ? It's all a mistake. We'll have you taken back to Prague. Sorry there's been a misunderstanding."

" Don't mention it," said Mr. Janik magnanimously. " I know the chauffeur's going to shoot me on the way back and then bury me in the woods. I don't mind. Silly ass that I was, I forgot to tell my address and this is what comes of it."

" You're boozed, aren't you ? " inquired the stranger with a certain relief.

" Partly," agreed Mr. Janik. " You see, I've had supper with a man named Meyer, from Dresden. I'm Janik, my line's wholesale paper and cellulose," he introduced himself, sitting on the stairs. " It's an old firm, founded by my grandfather."

" You go and sleep it off," the stranger advised him. " And when you have slept it off, you won't even remember that—hm, we disturbed you like this."

" Quite right," remarked Mr. Janik with dignity. " You go and sleep it off, too. Where can I get a bed ? "

" At home," said the stranger. " The chauffeur'll drive you home. Just let me help you to get up."

" I can manage," demurred Mr. Janik. " I'm not so tight as you. You go and sleep it off. Chauffeur, drive me to Bubeneč."

The car started off on the way back ; and Mr. Janik, with

a foxy twinkle in his eye, noticed where they were taking him from.

The next morning he telephoned to police-headquarters and gave an account of his adventure the previous night. " Mr. Janik," a voice from headquarters answered him after a moment's silence. " We're highly interested in this. I wonder if you'd mind coming here at once."

When Mr. Janik arrived, four gentlemen, with the tall, thick-set person at their head, were waiting for him. Mr. Janik had to tell them once more what had happened and whom he had seen. " The number of the car was NXX 705," added the thick-set gentleman. " A private car. Of the six persons whom Mr. Janik recognized, three are new to me. Gentlemen, I'll leave you now. Mr. Janik, come with me."

Mr. Janik, feeling very small, sat in the large office of the thick-set gentleman, who paced to and fro very deep in thought. " Mr. Janik," he said at last, " the first thing I have to say to you is : not a word to anyone about this. There are State secrets involved, do you understand ? "

Mr. Janik nodded silently. Good heavens, he thought to himself, what the dickens have I landed into now ?

" Mr. Janik," said the thick-set man suddenly, " I don't want to flatter you, but we need your services. You've got a lucky hand. People talk about method, but a detective who isn't devilish lucky isn't the slightest use. We need people with a lucky hand. We've got plenty of grit ourselves, but we'd give a good deal for the chance of a lucky fluke. Look here, you join us."

" And what about my business ? " murmured Mr. Janik, quite abashed.

" Your partner can look after that. It'd be a downright shame not to make proper use of that gift of yours. Well, what do you say ? "

" I'll—I'll have to think it over," stammered the luckless Mr. Janik. " I'll come to see you in a week's time . . . and if I'm really competent . . . I can't say yet. I'll come back again."

" All right," said the thick-set man, giving him a tremendous handshake. " You needn't be doubtful about yourself. Good day ! "

Before the week was over Mr. Janik turned up again. " Well, here I am," he chuckled, beaming all over his face.

" Have you made up your mind ? " asked the thick-set man.

" I should just think I have," said Mr. Janik with a sigh of relief. " And I've come to tell you that it's no go and I'm no good for the job."

" Nonsense. Why ever not ? "

" Just imagine," chortled Mr. Janik, " that my manager's been robbing me for the past five years and I never smelt a rat. That's the sort of idiot I am ! Well, a fine detective I'd make, wouldn't I ? Thank goodness ! For five years I was hobnobbing with a swindler and never saw through him. So you can judge for yourself how useless I'd be. And I was beginning to get quite nervous about it, too. By Jove ! I'm glad that nothing's going to come of it. Well, I suppose this is where I get out, eh ? Many thanks ! "

E

The Selvin Case

"HM, MY GREATEST success, I mean, the success which gave me the greatest pleasure——" said, in a reminiscent tone, old Leonard Unden, great poet, Nobel prize-winner, and so forth. "My young friends, at my age a man doesn't care a rap about laurels, ovations, women and such-like lunacy, especially when for years and years they've been a thing of the past. While a man's young he enjoys it all and he'd be a fool if he didn't. The only drawback is that while he's young he can't afford to enjoy anything. Life really ought to go in the reverse direction ; first of all, a man'd be old and he'd do plenty of useful work because he isn't fit for anything else ; it wouldn't be until later on that he'd arrive at youth so as to enjoy the fruits of his long life. You see how an old man goes rambling on. What was I going to talk about ? Oh yes, what was my greatest success. Well, I'll tell you : it wasn't any of my plays or any of my books, although there was a time when my books were really read. No, my greatest success was the Selvin case.

"Of course, you can't be expected to know what it was all about. Why, it must be twenty-six—no, it was twenty-nine years ago. Yes, it was twenty-nine years ago when one fine day a little white-haired old lady, dressed in black, came to see me.

"And before I could ask her, with that courtesy of mine which used to be so much appreciated then, what it was she wanted—wallop, she was kneeling down in front of me on the ground and had burst out crying. I don't know what it is, but I can't stand seeing a woman cry.

" ' You are a poet,' said the old lady when I had quietened her a little. ' I implore you, for the sake of your love for your fellow-men, save my son. No doubt you have read in the papers about Frank Selvin—— '

" I think I must have looked like a bearded baby then. Although I read the papers I hadn't noticed anything about Frank Selvin. Anyhow, as far as I could make out from what she was saying amid her sobbing and wailing, it was like this : Her only son, Frank Selvin, twenty-two years old, had just been sentenced to penal servitude for life on a charge of having murdered and attempted to rob his Aunt Sophie. What made things worse in the eyes of the jury was that he refused to admit having committed the crime.

" ' But he's innocent,' lamented Mrs. Selvin. ' I swear to you he's innocent. On that terrible evening he said to me : *Mother, I've got a headache, I'm going for a stroll on the common.* That's why he can't prove his alibi. Who'd take any notice of a young fellow at night, even if they'd happened to see him ? My Franky was rather a reckless boy, but you were young once yourself. Just fancy, he's only twenty-two ! How can they ruin a young man's whole life like that ? '

" And so on. I tell you, if you'd seen that broken-hearted, white-haired mother you'd have realized, just as I did at the time, that one of the most appalling ordeals is to pity a person when you're powerless to do anything for them. Well, at all events, I vowed to her that I'd do everything I possibly could and I'd spare no efforts until I'd got to the bottom of the matter ; also, that I believed in her son's innocence. When the poor old thing started blessing me it was all I could do not to kneel in front of her myself. You know what a fool it makes you look when anyone sheds gratitude upon you as if you were a little tin god.

" Well and good. From that moment onwards I took up

the case of Frank Selvin and threw myself heart and soul into it. Of course, first of all I went through a verbatim report of the trial. I tell you, never have I come across a trial that had been conducted in such a slapdash manner ; the thing was a downright scandal. The case itself was quite a simple one : One night, the servant of the Aunt Sophie in question, a certain Anne Solar, aged fifty and mentally deficient, heard someone moving about in Aunt Sophie's room. She went to see why her mistress was not asleep, and on entering the bedroom she saw that the window was wide open and she caught a glimpse of a man's form jumping out of the window into the garden. Thereupon she began to scream the house down, and when the neighbours arrived with a light they found Miss Sophie lying on the floor, strangled with her own handkerchief. The wardrobe where she used to keep her money had been broken open and part of the linen scattered about ; the money was still there ; evidently at that moment the servant had disturbed the murderer. Well, such were the facts of the case.

" The next day Frank Selvin was arrested. The servant, it appeared, had recognized the young gentleman when he was jumping out of the window. It was ascertained that he was not at home at that particular time ; he had returned home about half an hour later and had gone straight to bed. Further, it turned out that the young fool was in debt. Further, some chatterbox of an old woman had come forward to say with much ado that some time before the murder Aunt Sophie had told her in confidence that her nephew Frank had been there to try to get her to lend him some money ; when she refused—she was a shockingly stingy person, by the way —Frank had said : *Just you look out, something's going to happen that'll make people stare.* That was all, as far as Frank was concerned.

" And now, just consider the trial itself. It lasted, from

start to finish, half a day. Frank Selvin simply stated that
he was innocent, that he'd been for a walk, that he'd gone
straight home to bed. None of the witnesses was cross-
examined. Frank's counsel—he undertook the job without
payment, as Mrs. Selvin couldn't afford to pay for a proper
defence—was an easy-going old fool whose only argument
was to insist how young his scapegrace of a client was, and
with tears in his eyes he begged the kind-hearted gentlemen
of the jury to be indulgent. The public prosecutor polished
his job off very promptly, too ; he bullied the jury for having
acquitted two prisoners just before Frank Selvin's case had
come on. Where, he demanded, would society end up, if
every crime met with protection in the bland laxity and
lenience of juries ? It seems that the jury were alive to this
argument and wanted to show that there must be no com-
plaints about their laxity and lenience ; so they decided,
by eleven votes to one, that Frank Selvin was guilty of
murder. And that was the whole case.

" Now, let me tell you that when I had ascertained these
particulars I felt absolutely desperate. It fairly made my
blood boil, although I'm no lawyer or, rather, precisely
because I'm no lawyer. Just you imagine : the Crown
witness is mentally deficient ; on top of that, she's
nearly fifty years old and thus evidently nearing the change
of life, which under the circumstances was likely to make her
less trustworthy. It was at night that she had seen the form
in the window ; as I found out later, the night had been
warm but very dark ; so she couldn't have recognized the
man with any degree of certainty. In the darkness the
height of a man cannot be properly distinguished : I tested
that very thoroughly for myself. And, to crown all, the
woman detested young Frank Selvin, in a manner which
was nothing short of hysterical, because he used to make
fun of her. It seems that he called her ' white-elbowed

Hebe,' which for some reason or other she took as a mortal insult.

" Another point : Aunt Sophie hated her sister, Mrs. Selvin, and actually they were not on speaking terms ; the old maid used to call Frank's mother all sorts of names. If Aunt Sophie said that Frank had threatened her at all, it might very well be one of those old-maidish spiteful remarks which she passed with the set purpose of disparaging her sister. As regards Frank, he was a young fellow of average ability ; he was a clerk in some office or other; he had a sweetheart to whom he wrote sentimental letters and bad verses, and he fell into debt through no real fault of his own, for he was so mawkish that he took to drink. His mother, poor woman, was a paragon of goodness, afflicted with cancer, poverty and sorrow. Well, that was how things looked on a closer inspection.

" Of course, you don't know what I was like then, in my heyday ; when once my temper was roused, there was no holding me. What I then did was to write a series of articles to the papers entitled ' The Case of Frank Selvin ' ; point by point I showed how untrustworthy the witnesses were, especially the Crown witness ; I analysed the discrepancies in evidence and the biased character of some of the depositions ; I proved how absurd it was to suppose that the Crown witness could have recognized the culprit; I demonstrated the absolute incompetence of the judge and the uncouth demagogy in the speech of the public prosecutor. But that was not enough for me ; while I was about it I began to attack the administration of justice as a whole, the penal code, the jury system, the whole callous and selfish order of society. Don't ask me about the row that it caused ; at that time I already had some sort of a name, the young generation took my side ; in fact, one evening there was a regular demonstration in front of the law courts. Then young

Selvin's counsel came rushing round to see me. He was terribly upset about what he considered a grievous blunder on my part ; he said that he had already lodged an appeal against the verdict and that Selvin's sentence would undoubtedly have been commuted to a few years' imprisonment, but now the court of appeal could not be expected to yield to the mob and would therefore dismiss his appeal. I told the estimable barrister that I was not concerned only about Selvin's case, but I had espoused the cause of truth and justice.

" Selvin's counsel was right ; the appeal was dismissed, but the judge was pensioned off. My word, then I let myself go with a vengeance. I tell you, even to-day, I regard what I did then as a holy war for justice. Why, you can see for yourselves that there have been plenty of reforms since then, and you must admit, you know, that a little of the credit for them is due to me. Selvin's case found its way into newspapers all over the world. I made speeches to workmen in public-houses and to delegates from all sorts of countries at international congresses.

" ' Revise Selvin's Sentence ' was, in its time, as favourite an international slogan as, let us say, ' No More War ' or ' Votes for Women.' When Selvin's mother died, seventeen thousand people followed the coffin of the little desiccated old lady, and above her open grave I made a speech such as I have never made before or since ; inspiration, you know, is a weird and wonderful thing.

" I waged that war for seven years, and that war was the making of me. It was not my books, but the Selvin case, which gained me a world-wide reputation. I know they call me the Voice of Conscience, the Knight of Truth, or whatever else it may be ; some of these things will be on my tombstone, too. No doubt for fourteen years or so after my death the school reading-books will tell how Leonard Unden fought for truth ; then even that will be forgotten.

" In the seventh year the Crown witness, Anne Solar, died ; before her death she made a statement and amid much weeping confessed that her conscience was troubling her ; she had, she said, given false evidence at the trial ; she could not truthfully say that the murderer in the window was Frank Selvin. The priest, a well-meaning man, brought this along to me. By that time I had shrewder ideas about the way of the world and so I didn't take the story to the newspapers. Instead of that, I sent the good priest to the legal authorities. Within a week orders were given for Frank Selvin to be re-tried. Within a month Frank Selvin faced another jury ; the most prominent counsel pulverized the indictment free of charge ; whereupon the public prosecutor recommended the jury to acquit Frank Selvin ; and the jury brought in a unanimous verdict that Frank Selvin was not guilty.

" Yes, that was the greatest triumph of my life. None of my other successes caused me such pure gratification— and, at the same time, a sort of empty feeling. To tell the truth, I began to miss the Selvin case—it had left a gap in my mind. On the day after the trial the maid came and told me that there was a man who wanted to speak to me.

" ' I am Frank Selvin,' said the man, and stood in the doorway. And I felt—I don't know how to express it to you—but it was a bit of a disappointment for me that this Selvin of mine looked like—well, a turf agent ; rather stout and pasty-faced, with the beginnings of baldness; somewhat sweaty and much more than somewhat commonplace ; moreover, he smelt of beer.

" ' Great and illustrious artist,' stammered Frank Selvin (just fancy, he called me ' great and illustrious artist '—I could have kicked him !), ' I have come to thank you as my greatest benefactor.' It looked as if he had learnt it off by heart. ' I owe my whole life to you. All words of gratitude are weak——'

" ' Not at all,' I said to him hastily ; ' that was my duty. Once I was certain that you had been wrongly condemned—'

" Frank Selvin shook his head. ' No, sir,' he said mournfully. ' I couldn't lie to my benefactor. I killed the old woman right enough.'

" ' Then in the name of goodness,' I burst forth, ' why the deuce didn't you say so in court ? '

" Frank Selvin gazed at me reproachfully. ' No, sir,' he said, ' I was entitled to do that. The defendant is entitled to plead not guilty, isn't he ? '

" I must admit that this bowled me over.

" ' Well, what do you want of me now ? ' I snapped at him.

" ' I've just come to thank you for your noble generosity,' said Mr. Selvin in a woebegone voice which he evidently regarded as registering emotion. ' You took the part of my poor old mother, too. God bless you, noble poet ! '

" ' Get out ! ' I yelled. I was furious. The fellow flew downstairs like a shot. Three weeks later he stopped me in the street ; he was slightly drunk. I couldn't get rid of him ; for a long time I couldn't make out what he wanted, till he buttonholed me and explained matters. He said I'd messed things up for him ; if I hadn't written about his case, the appeal court would have given a hearing to his counsel's arguments and he, Mr. Selvin, wouldn't have spent seven years in prison for nothing. I ought, he said, at least to show some consideration for his reduced circumstances for which I was responsible through having meddled with his trial. To cut a long story short, I had to slip some money into his hand. ' God bless you for your kindness,' said Mr. Selvin in conclusion, with moist eyes.

" On the second occasion he approached me more threaten-ingly. He said I had made my way in the world on the strength of his case ; I had gained fame simply and solely by taking up his cause ; and so why should he get nothing out of it ? I was entirely unable to persuade him that I owed him nothing in the way of commission ; I just gave him more money.

" From that time onwards he would pay me a call at shorter and shorter intervals ; he would sit down on the sofa and sigh about the remorse he was suffering at having made away with the old woman. ' I'm going to give myself up,' he said gloomily, ' but it'll land you in a fine old mess. Still, I don't see how else I'm to get any peace of mind.' I tell you, these fits of remorse must be pretty awful, judging by what I kept paying that fellow so as he could go on bearing them. Finally I bought him a ticket to America ; whether he got any peace of mind there I don't know.

" Well, that was the greatest success of my life. My young friends, when you write an obituary notice of Leonard Unden, say that by the Selvin case he engraved his name in golden letters, and so on ; thanks be to him for evermore."

The Coupon

*　*　*

ON THAT hot August evening the café by the river was crowded ; and the consequence was that Minnie and Joe had to sit down at a table which was already occupied by a gentleman with a bushy, drooping moustache. " You don't mind if we sit here ? " said Joe, and the gentleman merely shook his head. (What a horrid man, said Minnie to herself, to have sitting just at our table.) So first of all, Minnie with the attitude of a duchess sat down on the chair which Joe wiped for her with his handkerchief. And then, immediately afterwards, she took out her powder-puff and powdered her nose to make quite certain that it wouldn't get shiny in the heat. Just as she was taking out the powder-puff, a crumpled slip of paper fell from her handbag. Thereupon the gentleman with the moustache bent down and picked up the small slip. " You should keep that, young lady," he said in gloomy tones.

Minnie turned red, first of all because a strange gentleman had spoken to her, and then because she was annoyed at having turned red. " Thank you," she said, and turned briskly to Joe. " That's the coupon from the shop where I bought my stockings."

" Just so," said the melancholy man. " And you never can tell what use it might be, young lady."

Joe considered it his duty as a gentleman to have his say too. " What's the good of keeping useless bits of paper ? " he remarked, without looking at the strange gentleman. " They only fill your pockets with litter."

" That doesn't matter," observed the man with the

73

moustache. " Sometimes a thing like that's more valuable than you'd think."

Minnie's face assumed a strained expression. (The horrid man's going to poke his nose into our conversation. Why ever didn't we sit somewhere else?) Joe decided to put a stop to it. " How do you mean, more valuable? " he asked coldly, and raised his eyebrows. (How well it suits him, noted Minnie with satisfaction.)

" As a clue," muttered the horrid man, and by way of introduction added, " You see, I belong to the detective force. Souček's my name. We've just had a case like that," he remarked with a wave of the hand. " People can never tell what they're carrying in their pockets."

" What case? " Joe couldn't help asking. (Minnie caught the glance of a young man at the next table. All right, Joe, I'll pay you out for talking to strangers.)

" Why, the woman they found near Roztyly," said the man with the moustache, and lapsed into silence.

Minnie suddenly became interested, most likely because there was a woman in the case. " What woman? " she blurted out.

" Why, the one they found out there," muttered Mr. Souček of the detective force, evasively, and in some slight embarrassment he fished a cigarette out of his pocket. Whereupon something quite unforeseen occurred : Joe hastily dived into his pocket, produced his lighter, and gave the man a light.

" Thanks," said Mr. Souček, evidently appreciative of the favour. " You know, some reapers found a woman's body in a cornfield between Roztyly and Krč," he explained, thus showing that he was grateful for the favour and was returning it.

" I never heard anything about that," said Minnie with

startled eyes. " Joe, do you remember when we were at Krč ? And what had happened to the woman ? "

" She'd been strangled," remarked Mr. Souček dryly. "She still had the cord round her neck. I can't very well say what she looked like, in front of the young lady here. You know, it was in July and she'd been lying there close on two months——" Mr. Souček disgustedly puffed out a mouthful of smoke. " You've got no idea what anyone looks like when they're in that state. Why, their own mother wouldn't know 'em. And then the flies——" Mr. Souček shook his head mournfully. " Young lady, once the skin's gone, there ain't much beauty left. And it's a deuce of a job to find out who it is. As long as they've got nose and eyes, there's still a chance. But when they've been lying in the sun for over a month——"

" But there must have been some initials on the corpse," suggested Joe with the air of an expert.

" No such luck," muttered Mr. Souček. " Single girls don't usually have initials on them because they says to themselves, it ain't worth while; I'll be getting married soon. No, there wasn't no initials on the woman."

" And how old was she ? " inquired Minnie with close interest.

" The doctor said, about twenty-five. By her teeth and so on, you see. And judging by her clothes she might have been a working-girl or a servant, but most likely a servant, because she had a sort of countrified petticoat. And besides, if it had been a working-girl, there'd have probably been some inquiries after her, because working-girls generally stay for some time in the same job or in the same lodgings. But once a servant changes her job, nobody knows anything about her and nobody cares. That's the funny thing about servants, ain't it ? So we made up our minds that if nobody had been inquiring after her for two months, then she was most likely a servant. But the chief thing about it was the coupon."

"What coupon?" asked Joe eagerly. For he doubtless felt within him the heroic makings of a detective, a Canadian backwoodsman, a sea captain, or something of that sort, and his face took on that concentrated and energetic look which is all part of the business.

"Well, it was like this," began Mr. Souček, and gazed moodily at the ground. "There was nothing whatever found on her. The chap who did her in had taken everything away that was likely to be worth anything at all. But in her left hand she still held a strap that had been torn away from a handbag, and the hand-bag without the strap was found a little way off among the corn. He probably had wanted to drag the hand-bag away from her, but when the strap broke, it wasn't any good to him, so he threw it away among the corn. But first of all he took everything out of it, see? So all that was left in the hand-bag was a tram-ticket of route No. 7, which had got covered up in a sort of fold, and a coupon from a china-shop, marking a purchase to the value of fifty-five crowns. That's all we found on her."

"But the cord round her neck," said Joe. "That's what you ought to have followed up."

Mr. Souček shook his head. "That was only just a piece of clothes-line. That wasn't any good. We'd got absolutely nothing but the tram-ticket and the coupon. Of course, we had a notice put into the papers to say that the body of a woman had been found, age about twenty-five years, grey petticoat and striped blouse, and if any girl in service has been missing for about two months, kindly report same to police. We got over a hundred people coming forward with statements. You see, May's the month when these servant-girls mostly change their jobs, although nobody knows why.

But none of these statements led anywhere. I tell you, it's no end of a job, following up a lot of particulars like that," said Mr. Souček sadly. "You get a skivvy who was in service at Dejvice, say, and before you can find traces of her again at Vršovice or Košíře, why, it means running about all day long. And then it's all no use. The young hussy's alive and kicking, and has the cheek to laugh at you into the bargain. That's a nice piece they're playing now," he remarked, moving his head to and fro with approval, and keeping time with Wagner's Valkyrie music, which the band was playing with all its might and main. "Sort of sad, ain't it? I'm very fond of sad music. That's why I attend all the big funerals, to nab the pickpockets there."

"But the murderer must have left some clues," observed Joe.

"Do you see that chap there?" remarked Mr. Souček with interest. "He goes after the offertory boxes in churches. I'd like to know what he's up to here. No, the murderer never left no clues. But let me tell you this much, that if you find a girl murdered, you can bet your life it was her sweetheart who did it. That's how it turns out," he said moodily. "Not that you need worry your head about that, young lady. So we wanted to know who'd done her in. But first of all we had to find out who she was. That was the hard part of the business."

"But the police have got their own methods for things like that," said Joe waveringly.

"Oh, of course," agreed Mr. Souček glumly. "The same sort of method like, for instance, looking for a pin in a haystack. I tell you, you want lots of patience for a job like that. I like reading these here detective tales with all their talk about microscopes and what not. But what good would a microscope be to you for finding out about that poor girl? It'd be all right if you wanted to have a peep at this here fat worm, as happy as can be, taking his young 'uns out for a walk. No offence meant, young lady, but it always riles me when I hear them talking about method. You see, it ain't like reading a story-book and just guessing how it's all going to end up. It's more like as if someone was to give you a story-book and say : Well, here you are, you've got to read this word by word, and when you find the word *although*, just make a note of the page. That's the kind of job it is, see ? No methods or smartness is going to help you there. What you got to do is to read on and on, and when you've finished you find out that the word *although* ain't in the book at all. Or you got to go trapesing about from one end of Prague to the other and discover the whereabouts of a hundred or so girls named Angelica or Maria, so that by detective work of that kind you can settle the fact that none of them's been murdered. That's what they ought to write about," he remarked in dissatisfied tones, " and not about the Queen of Sheba's stolen pearl necklace. Because, you see, when all's said and done, it's a sound and solid piece of work."

" And how did you set about it then ? " asked Joe, who was certain beforehand that he would have set about it differently.

" How we set about it ? " repeated Mr. Souček pensively. " Why, first of all we had to have something to go upon, didn't we ? Well, for a start we had that tram-ticket of route No. 7. Now suppose that this girl, if she was a servant, that is, was in service somewhere near the tram-line ; it may not mean anything, because she might have gone for a ride that way just by chance. Only we've got to take something for granted, if we're going to make a start at all, ain't we ? The only thing is that, as it happens, route No. 7 goes from one end of Prague to the other. So that's no good and we can't do anything with it. Then there was that coupon.

That showed at any rate that some time back the girl had bought goods to the value of fifty-five crowns in a china-shop. So we went to the shop."

" And did they remember her there ? " Minnie gasped.

" Remember her, young lady ? " growled Mr. Souček. " Not they. But Mr. Mejzlik, he's the superintendent of our division, went and inquired what you could buy there for fifty-five crowns. All sorts of things, they told him, according to how many articles there were. But the only single article they sell for exactly fifty-five crowns is a tea-pot, big enough for one person. ' Well, let me have one then,' says our superintendent, ' but make it a job lot so that it won't cost so much.' So then the superintendent sends for me and says : ' Look here, Souček, here's a job for you. Suppose this girl was in service. Girls like that are always breaking something, and when she's done it for the third time, her mistress says to her, you clumsy thing you, now you'll have to pay for it out of your own money. So the girl goes and buys just one article to replace the one she's broken. And the only thing that'd cost fifty-five crowns would be a tea-pot like this one.' ' That's damn dear,' I says to him. And he says, ' My good man, that's just the point. First of all it shows why the girl kept the coupon. It meant a mint of money to her and maybe she thought that some day or other her mistress would let her have it back. And then there's another thing. This is a tea-pot for one person. That means that either the girl was in service with a person on their own, or else her mistress had a person on their own as a lodger and they used to have their breakfast brought to them in this tea-pot. And this person on their own was most likely a female, because a man would hardly buy such a fine, expensive tea-pot, would he ? Men don't generally notice what they're drinking out of. The most likely thing of all would be that it was an old maid, because when you get a spinster like that, in lodgings, she's always very anxious to have something nice of her own, and so she'll buy some needlessly expensive article.' "

" That's quite right," exclaimed Minnie. " I've got such a beautiful little flower-vase, Joe ! "

" There you are," said Mr. Souček. " But you haven't kept the coupon belonging to it, have you ? So then the superintendent says : ' Now then, Souček, let's do a little more guessing. It's all damned uncertain, but we've got to begin somewhere. Well now, look here ; the person who can afford to spend fifty-five crowns on a tea-pot ain't likely to live at Žižkov.' (You see, Mr. Mejzlik had still got his eye on tram-route No. 7, that the tram-ticket belonged to.) ' There ain't many lodgers in central Prague, and the ones who live on the Malá Strana only drink coffee. If you ask me, I should say it would most likely be someone living between the Hradčany and Dejvice. In fact,' he says, ' I'm inclined to think that the lady who drinks tea from an English tea-pot like that can hardly live anywhere except in one of those small houses with a garden. You know, Souček, that's the modern English style of place. You see, our Mr. Mejzlik, he sometimes has crazy ideas of that sort. Now I'll tell you what, Souček,' he says, ' you take this tea-pot and make inquiries in that part of the town to see whether any better-class spinsters are lodging in the neighbourhood ; and if any of them should happen to have a tea-pot like this, ask whether a servant left her landlady some time in last May. It's a damned weak clue, but it's worth trying. Now run along, old boy, this is your job now.'

" Well, you know, I've got no particular liking for all this guess-work ; a good, straightforward detective ain't a star-gazer or a fortune-teller. It ain't no part of a detective's job to do a lot of fancy thinking. Of course, sometimes they manage to hit on the right thing by chance, but chance ain't what I call honest work. Now that tram-ticket and that tea-pot, they're at least something I can see ; but all the rest of it is just a . . . a figment of the imagination," said Mr. Souček, rather shame-faced to be heard using so learned a phrase. " So I set about it in my own way. I went from house to house in the neighbourhood and asked whether they hadn't got a tea-pot of that sort there. And believe me or believe me not, in the forty-seventh house I went to, the servant says, ' Lawks ! why the lady who lodges with the mistress has got a tea-pot just like that.' So I had myself announced to the landlady. She was a general's widow and let out two rooms to ladies. One of the ladies, a Miss Jakoubek, a teacher of English, had just such a tea-pot. ' Ma'am,' I says, ' didn't one of your maids leave you some time in May ? ' ' Yes,' says the landlady, ' that's right, we called her Mařka, but I don't remember now what her other name was.' ' And did she break anything belonging to your lodger before she went ? ' ' Yes,' says the landlady, ' she did, and she had to replace it out of her own money ; but my goodness me, how do you know about it ? ' ' Ah, ma'am, you see we get to know everything.'

" Well, after that it was plain sailing. First of all I discovered the maid that this Mařka was pally with—it's a funny thing, a servant-girl is never pally with more than one other servant-girl, but she tells her everything—and I found out from her that the girl's name was Marie Pařízek and she came from Dřevíč. But what I wanted to know most of all was who this Mařka was walking out with. She said it was a fellow named Franta ; she didn't know what this Franta was, but she remembered that she'd once been together with the two of them in a dance-hall called Eden, and there another fellow had called out to this Franta : ' What cheer, Ferda ! ' Well then, this was handed over to a Mr. Frýba in our section—you know, he's the one who's got all these

aliases at his fingers' ends.   And Frýba said straight away :
' Franta alias Ferda, that's probably the chap who calls
himself Kroutil, but his real name's Pastyřík ; he hails from
Košíře, he does.   I'll go and fetch him, but there'll have to
be two of us for that job.'   So I went with him, although
that ain't really my line of work.   We collared him while he
was with his girl ; he got nasty about it and wanted to shoot.
Then Superintendent Matička took charge of him.   I tell
you, nobody knows how he does it, but in sixteen hours he
managed to make this chap Franta or Pastyřík own up to
everything, how he'd strangled this Marie Pařízek in a hedge
and robbed her of a few crowns, just when she'd left the
place where she was in service.   You see, he'd promised to
marry her—they all do that," he added gloomily.

Minnie shuddered.   " Joe," she whispered, " isn't it
awful ! "

" Not now it ain't," said Mr. Souček solemnly.   " But
you know it was awful when we were standing by her body
in that field and found nothing but the coupon and the tram-
ticket.   A couple of paltry, useless scraps of paper like that
—and yet we managed to avenge that poor girl.   As I said,
you ought never to throw anything away, never ; even the
most useless thing may prove to be a clue or evidence.   No,
sir, you never can tell what important things you may be
carrying in your pocket."

Minnie's startled eyes were full of tears.   In a warm burst
of affection she turned to Joe and her moist hand dropped
the coupon, which all this time she had been nervously
rolling into a pellet between her fingers.   Joe did not notice
this because he was gazing at the stars.   But Mr. Souček, of
the police force, noticed it and smiled sadly and compre-
hendingly.

Oplatka's End

★ ★ ★

A T THREE o'clock in the morning P.C. Krejčik noticed
that the shutters of a baker's shop at No. 17 Neklanova
Street were half raised. He accordingly rang the door-
bell, and although he was not on duty, he peeped under the
shutter to see if there was anyone in the shop. At this
moment a man dashed out of the shop, fired a bullet into
Krejčik's stomach at close range and made his escape.

P.C. Bartoš, who was patrolling Jeronymova Street,
which was his prescribed beat at this hour, heard the shot
and came running up towards it. At the corner of Neklanova Street he very nearly collided with the fugitive ; but
before he could shout " Stop ! " a shot was fired and P.C.
Bartoš collapsed mortally wounded.

The street was now astir with a screeching of police-
whistles : the mounted patrols came galloping up from the
whole of that area, three men arrived at the double from the
police station, buttoning their tunics as they ran ; after a few
minutes a car rattled along from headquarters and from it a
police superintendent jumped out ; at this instant P.C.
Bartoš was already dead and Krejčik was dying, as he
clutched at his stomach.

By the morning about twenty arrests had been made ;
this was done at random, because nobody had seen the
murderer ; but in the first place the police somehow had to
avenge the deaths of two of their men, and, besides, it is
usual to do this ; the supposition is that by some divine
stroke of luck someone among those arrested will prove to
be the wanted man. At headquarters cross-examinations
were going on uninterruptedly all day and all night ; pale
and jaded wrongdoers, known to the police, were writhing

on the rack of endless cross-questionings, but they quaked still more at the thought of what would happen when a few constables took them in hand after the cross-examination ; for the whole of the police force was seething with a dark and awesome rage. The murder of P.C. Bartoš had violated that rather free-and-easy relationship which exists between the professional policeman and the professional criminal ; if he had merely fired, that wouldn't have mattered so much, but you don't shoot even dumb animals in the stomach.

By the next night, towards the early hours of the morning, every policeman, however remote his beat, knew that Oplatka had done it. This had been blabbed out by one of those arrested as suspects : Oh yes, Valta said as how Oplatka had done in those two chaps in Neklanova Street, and he'd settle some more of 'em, that he would ; it was all the same to him because he'd got consumption. Very well, then, it was Oplatka.

That same night Valta was arrested, then Oplatka's sweetheart and three fellows belonging to Oplatka's gang ; but none of them could or would say where Oplatka was to be found. How many policemen and plain-clothes men had been sent to track Oplatka down, is another matter ; but apart from that, every policeman, as soon as he had gone off duty, went home and gulped down some thin coffee, muttered something to his wife, pulled himself together and started off on his own to look for Oplatka. Of course, everybody knew Oplatka ; he was a green-faced little shrimp with a scraggy neck.

At eleven o'clock at night P.C. Vrzal, who had gone off duty at nine, hastily got into plain clothes and told his wife that he was just going to have a look round in the street, came across a weedy man near the Paradise Garden who seemed to be keeping well in the shadow. P.C. Vrzal, although he was unarmed and off duty, went a little nearer to have a look ; but when he was within three yards of him, the man thrust his hand in his pocket, shot Vrzal in the stomach and took to his heels. P.C. Vrzal clutched at his stomach and started running after him ; when he had run a hundred yards he collapsed ; but by that time the police whistles had started shrilling and quite a number of men were hot-foot after the shadow. Behind Rieger Park a few shots were heard ; a quarter of an hour later several cars, festooned with policemen, were racing along towards upper Žižkov and patrols consisting of three or four men crept through the buildings in course of construction in that quarter. Towards one o'clock the bang of a pistol-shot was heard behind the Olšany pond ; someone who was on the run fired at a youth who had just left his girl and was on his way home, but missed him. At two o'clock in the morning a posse of policemen and detectives encircled a patch of waste ground containing some disused kilns, and step by step drew closer. It began to drizzle. Towards morning there was a rumour that behind Malešice someone had fired at a toll-keeper who had his booth there ; the toll-keeper had started running after him, but then he had wisely decided that it was no business of his. Evidently Oplatka had slipped away into the fields.

Some sixty men in helmets and bowler-hats were returning from the disused kilns, wet through and so fuming with impotent rage that they could have wept. Good heavens, how infuriating it was ! Here was the ruffian who had slaughtered three members of the police force, Bartoš, Krejčik and Vrzal, and now he was running right into the clutches of the gendarmes. *We* have the prior claim, opined the police in uniform and plain clothes, and now we've got to leave this wretched little shrimp of an Oplatka to the gendarmes. Look here, as he's been shooting our men, it's our job, isn't it ? We don't want these gendarme chaps poking their noses into it ; all they ought to do is to get into his way so that he can't go back to Prague.

The whole day there was a cold drizzle ; in the evening towards dusk Mrázek, a gendarme, was on his way from Čerčany, where he had gone to buy a battery for his wireless set, to Pyšely ; he was unarmed and was whistling to himself. As he was going along, he saw an undersized fellow in front of him ; there was nothing special about this, but the undersized fellow stopped, as if uncertain which way to go. Who can that be, said Mrázek to himself, and at that very instant he saw a flash and rolled over, clutching at his side.

That same evening, of course, the gendarmerie throughout the district was on the alert. " Look here, Mrázek," said Captain Honzátko to the dying man, " don't you worry about this. I give you my word that we'll collar the blackguard. It's that fellow Oplatka and I'll bet anything he's trying to get to Soběslav, because that's his birthplace. Goodness knows why these fellows make for their hometown when their number's up. Well, old chap, give me your hand ; I promise you we'll settle his hash for him, by hook or crook." Václav Mrázek made an attempt at a smile ; he was thinking of his three children, but then in his mind's eye he saw the gendarmes drawing closer and closer on all sides . . . perhaps Toman of Černý Kostel would be among them . . . Závada of Votice certainly would . . . Rousek of Sázava would too, his chums, his chums . . . What a fine sight it will be, thought Václav Mrázek, all those gendarmes together. Then Mrázek smiled for the last time ; after that there was only some inhuman agony.

But what happened that night was that Sergeant Závada of Votice thought it would be a good idea to search the night train from Benešov ; who could tell, perhaps Oplatka was travelling in it ; by Jove though, would he risk getting into a train ? Lights flickered in the carriages ; the passengers were dozing on the seats, hunched together like weary animals. Sergeant Závada went from carriage to carriage and thought to himself, how the deuce am I to recognize a man I've never seen ? At that instant a yard away from him a fellow jumped up with his hat over his eyes, there was a loud report, and before the sergeant in the narrow corridor could unhitch his rifle from his shoulder, the weedy person was outside, brandishing a revolver. Sergeant Závada just had time to shout " Stop him ! " before he fell in a heap in the corridor of the carriage.

Meanwhile the fellow had jumped from the carriage and was running towards the goods trucks. There a railwayman named Hrůša was walking along with a lantern and saying to himself, well, as soon as No. 26 has left, I'll go and have a lie down in the lamp-shed. At this instant a man ran into him. Old Hrůša without wasting words tried to stop him from passing ; that's just a man's instinct. Then he saw a sort of flash and that was all ; even before No. 26 had left, old Hrůša was lying in the lamp-shed, but on a plank, and the railwaymen went to look at him with bare heads.

A few men ran panting after the escaping shadow, but it was too late ; by this time he had probably got across the railway-lines into the fields. But thence, from that flickering railway-station, from that cluster of scared people a wild panic swooped in a broad circle across the countryside, enwrapt in autumnal drowsiness. The people shrank into their cottages and scarcely dared to set foot in the doorway. There was a rumour that at such and such a place someone had seen a stranger of wild appearance ; he was either a lanky and haggard man, or else more of a short fellow in a leather coat ; a postman saw someone hiding behind a tree ; someone on the highroad had made signs to a carman named Lebeda to stop, but Lebeda had lashed at his horses and driven off. It was a fact that someone sobbing with fatigue had stopped a child on its way to school, and snatched away a little bag containing a slice of bread. " Give me that," the man had gasped and had then run off with the bread. As soon as this was known, the villagers had bolted their doors and scarcely breathed for fear ; the most they dared to do was to press their noses against the window-pane and gaze out with misgivings at the grey and desolate countryside.

But at the same time there was another concentrating movement which began to develop. From every direction the gendarmes arrived in ones and twos ; heaven knows where they all came from. " Good heavens, man," shouted Captain Honzátko at a gendarme from Cáslav, " what do you want here ? Who sent you here ? Do you think I need gendarmes from the whole of Bohemia to catch one gun-man ? Eh ? " The gendarme from Cáslav took off his helmet and scratched his neck in embarrassment. " Well, you see, sir," he said with an appealing glance, " Závada was a pal of mine—it wouldn't be fair to him if I wasn't in it, would it now ? " " Confound you fellows," thundered the captain, " that's what they all tell me. Close on fifty gendarmes have reported themselves to me without any orders— what am I to do with you ? " Captain Honzátko gnawed his moustache savagely. " All right, you'll be on duty along the highway here from the cross-roads to the woods ; tell Voldřich, the man from Benešov, that you've come to relieve him." " That's no go, sir," opined the gendarme from Cáslav sagaciously. " You see, sir, Voldřich he won't hear of me relieving him ; it stands to reason, don't it ? It'd be better if I was to take the woods from the edge up to that second road—who's on duty there ? " " Semerád from Veselka," growled the captain. " Now listen, you from Cáslav, and get this : on my responsibility you'll fire without warning, if you see anyone. No shilly-shallying, do you understand ? I'm not going to let my men be shot. Now, off you go."

Then the stationmaster arrived. " Well, sir," he said, " there's another thirty of 'em turned up." " Thirty what?" " Why," said the stationmaster, " railwaymen, of course. You know, it's all along of Hrůša. He was one of our men and so they've come to offer you their services." " Send them back," yelled the captain. " I don't need any civilians here." The stationmaster moved uneasily from one foot to the other. " You see, sir," he remarked soothingly, " they've come here all the way from Prague and Mezimosti. It's a good thing when they stick together like that. You know, they won't take no for an answer now that Oplatka's killed one of them. They've sort of got a right to it. So if I was you, sir, I'd do them the favour and take them on."

Captain Honzátko snarled that he wished to goodness they'd leave him alone. In the course of the day the broad circle gradually drew closer. That afternoon the nearest garrison headquarters telephoned to know whether any military reinforcements were needed. " No," snapped the captain disrespectfully ; " that's our job, and nobody else's." Meanwhile some members of the secret police had arrived from Prague ; they had a fearful row with the sergeant-major who was going to send them back neck and crop from the railway station. " What," fumed Inspector Holub, " you want to send us back ? He's killed three of our men and only two of yours, you swabs ! We're more entitled to him than you are, you tin-hatted chumps, you ! " Scarcely had this conflict been settled than a new one broke out on the other side of the circle, between the gendarmes and the gamekeepers. " Get out of our way," fumed the gendarmes. " This isn't a rabbit-hunt." " You be blowed," remarked the gamekeepers ; " these are our woods and we're entitled to walk here, ain't we ? " " Now come, come, you chaps, don't be so silly," said Rousek from Sázava, acting as a mediator ; " this is our job and nobody's got to interfere in it." " That's what you say," retorted the game-keepers. " But the kid that this fellow took the bread from is the Hůrka gamekeeper's little girl. We can't let that pass, so there you are."

That evening the circle was closed ; when darkness had fallen, each man heard the hoarse breathing of the man on his right and on his left and the squelch of footsteps in the sticky soil. " Halt ! " sped the word from man to man. " Don't move ! " The silence was heavy and awesome ; only every now and then there was a crunch of dry leafage in the darkness in the middle of the circle or a switch of rainfall ; only every now and then was heard the squelchy tread of a man tramping past or a metallic clatter perhaps of a rifle or a strap. Towards midnight someone in the darkness yelled " Halt ! " and fired a shot ; at that moment there was a queer grinding noise, and the muffled report of about thirty rifle-shots ; they all ran forward in that direction, but then there came a yell : " Get back! Nobody's to move a step." They got back into some sort of order and the circle was closed again ; but only now did they all fully realize that in the darkness before them a lost man was hiding at bay, on the alert for a chance to make a wild attack. A kind of uncontrollable shudder passed from man to man ; from time to time the heavy drip of water made a stir like a stealthy footstep. Good heavens, if only something could be seen ! Ye gods, if only it was light !

Day began to dawn mistily. Each man distinguished the outlines of the man next to him, marvelling that he had been so close to a human being. In the middle of the chain of men the contours of a dense thicket or spinney became visible (it was a covert for hares), but it was so quiet there, so utterly quiet—Captain Honzátko tugged feverishly at his moustache : damn it, we've got to go on waiting, or else——

" I'm going to have a look there," growled Holub ; the captain snorted. " You go," he said, turning to the nearest gendarme. Five men rushed into the thicket, there was a crackle of broken branches and sudden stillness. " Stay where you are," shouted Captain Honzátko to his men and moved slowly towards the copse. Then there emerged from the thicket the broad back of a gendarme dragging something, a huddled body, the feet of which were being held by a gamekeeper with a walrus moustache. Behind them Captain Honzátko, scowling and sallow, squeezed his way from the copse. " Lay him down here," he gasped, wiping his forehead ; he looked round, with an air of surprise at the wavering chain of men, scowled still more and shouted : " What are you staring at ? Dismiss ! "

In some embarrassment man after man straggled forward to the puny, hunched body by the hedge. So that was Oplatka ; the gaunt arm sticking out from the sleeve, the puny, greenish, rain-soaked face on the scraggy neck—ye gods, what a pitifully undersized specimen of a man, this poor wretch Oplatka ! Hello, he's been shot in the back, and here's a tiny wound behind one of his projecting ears, and here again . . . Four, five, seven of them had got him. Captain Honzátko, who was kneeling by the body, stood up and cleared his throat moodily ; then uneasily and almost timidly he raised his eyes—there stood a long, massive row of gendarmes, rifle on shoulder, the shining bayonets fixed ; good heavens, what strapping fellows, like tanks, and there they stood two-deep as if they were on parade, with bated breath. On the other side a black cluster of secret police, thick-set men one and all, their pockets bulging with a revolver ; then the railwaymen in blue uniforms, stocky and dogged ; then the gamekeepers in green, sinewy and bearded, with lanky bodies and brick-red faces. Why, it's like a public funeral, was the thought that flashed through the captain's mind ; they've formed a square, as if they had to fire a salute. Captain Honzátko gnawed at his lip in an unreasoning pang of torment. That midget lying on the ground, stark and bristly, an ailing crow who has been riddled with bullets, and here all these hunters—" Damn it all ! " shouted the captain, gritting his teeth, " haven't you got a sack or something ? Clear the body away ! "

Some two hundred men began to disperse in various directions ; they did not talk to each other, but only grumbled about the bad roads, and in reply to excited questions muttered sullenly, Aye, it's all up with him, and we've had enough of it. The gendarme who had been left on guard over the covered body snarled savagely at the loitering bumpkins : " What do you want ? There is nothing for you to stare at here. This is no business of yours."

At the district boundaries Rousek, the gendarme from Sázava, spat and quoth thus : " Damn this rotten weather ! I'd rather be out of it all, I can tell you. Good Lord, I only wish I could have got at that chap Oplatka all on my own, man to man ! "

The Farm Murder

★　★　★

"PRISONER AT the bar, stand up," said the judge. "You are charged with having murdered František Lebeda, your father-in-law; during the preliminary investigations you admitted that you deliberately struck him three times on the head with an axe, with intent to kill him. Now then, do you plead guilty?"

The peasant, who looked worn out with drudgery, trembled and gulped.

"No," he muttered.

"Did you kill him?"

"Yes."

"Then you plead guilty?"

"No."

The judge had the patience of an angel. "Look here, Vondráček," he said, "it's been shown that once before you tried to poison him; you put rat-poison in his coffee. Is that true?"

"Yes."

"That's a proof that you've had designs on his life for some considerable time. Do you understand me?"

The peasant sniffed and shrugged his shoulders in bewilderment. "It was all along of that there clover," he stammered. "He sold the clover, and I said to him, *Dad, you leave that clover be, I'm going to buy some rabbits—*"

"Wait a bit," interrupted the judge; "was that his clover or yours?"

"Why, his," mumbled the accused: "but what's he want clover for? So I said to him, *Dad, anyway, leave me the field where you've got the lucern*, but he says, *When I'm*

93

dead, Marka'll get it—that's my wife—*and then you do what you like with it, you greedy skinflint, you.*"

" So that's why you wanted to poison him ? "

" Why, yes."

" Because he called you names ? "

" No. It was all along of that there field. He said he was going to sell the field."

" But, my good man," burst out the judge, " it was his field, wasn't it ? Why shouldn't he sell it ? "

Vondráček gazed reproachfully at the judge. " Why, I've got a potato patch next to that field," he explained. " I bought it so as one day it could join the field, but he said : *What do I care about your patch, I'm going to sell the field to Joudal.*"

" So you lived on bad terms with each other," observed the judge.

" Why, yes," said Vondráček gloomily. " That was all along of the goat."

" What goat ? "

" He milked my goat dry. I said to him, *Dad, leave that goat alone, or else give us that bit of pasture by the stream.* But he let the pasture."

" And what did he do with the money ? " asked a jury-man.

" Why, he stored it up in a cash-box, of course," replied the accused sullenly. " *When I'm dead*, he said, *you'll get it*. But he wouldn't die, not him. And him over seventy, and all."

" So according to you, it was your father-in-law who was the cause of these disagreements ? "

" Yes," said Vondráček slowly. " He wouldn't give anything. *While I'm alive*, he said, *I'll manage things myself, so put that in your pipe and smoke it*. So I said to him, *Dad, if you was to buy a cow, I'd plough that field and it wouldn't have to be sold.* But he said, *When I'm dead, you can buy two cows, if you like, but I'm going to sell my bit of land to Joudal."*

" Look here, Vondráček," said the judge sternly, " didn't you kill him for the money that was in the cash-box ? "

" That was to buy the cow with," said Vondráček stubbornly. " We reckoned out that when he was dead we'd have a cow. You can't do without a cow on a farm, can you ? Where was I to get the manure from ? "

" Prisoner at the bar," the public prosecutor here intervened, " we are not concerned with a cow, but with a human life. Why did you kill your father-in-law ? "

" That was all along of the field."

" That's no answer."

" He wanted to sell the field——"

" But the money would have been yours after his death, just the same."

" Yes, but he wouldn't die," said Vondráček sulkily. " You see, your honour, if he'd died without any fuss like, I would never have done him any harm. All the village can prove that I treated him like my own father, can't you ? " he said, turning to the public. The body of the court, where half the village was present, rumbled with sounds of assent.

" Yes," said the judge solemnly, " and that's why you wanted to poison him, isn't it ? "

" Poison," muttered the accused. " Then he didn't ought to have sold that clover. Your honour, everyone'll tell you as how clover ought to be kept. That's not the way to manage a farm, is it ? "

There was a murmur of assent in the body of the court.

" Face me, prisoner at the bar," shouted the judge, " or I'll have your friends cleared out of the court. Tell us how the murder took place."

" Well," began Vondráček with deliberation, " it was on

G

a Sunday and I saw him talking to Joudal again. *Dad*, I said to him, *you mustn't sell that field so as I can't have it.* But he said, *It ain't likely I'm going to ask you about it, you clodhopper.* So I said to myself, *It's time something was done*, see. So I went to chop some wood."

" Was this the axe ? "

" Yes."

" Continue your story."

" In the evening I said to my wife : *You go and take the children to their aunt.* She started crying there and then : *Don't cry*, I said, *I'll have a talk with him first.* So then he came into the shed and says to me, *This is my axe, give it here !* And I told him as how he'd milked my goat dry. Then he tried to drag the axe away from me. So I hit at him."

" Why ? "

" It was all along of the field."

" And why did you hit him three times ? "

Vondráček shrugged his shoulders. " Well, you see, your honour, the likes of us are used to hard work."

" And then ? "

" Then I went to have a lie down."

" Did you sleep ? "

" No. I was reckoning how much the cow would cost and that I'd exchange the pasture for the strip by the roadside. Then it'd all be together."

" And your conscience didn't worry you ? "

" No. What worried me was that those fields wasn't together. And then the byre for the cow has got to be mended, that'll cost a tidy bit of money, too. Why, my father-in-law, he never even had a cart. I used to say to him, *Dad, may the Lord forgive you your sins, but this ain't the way to manage a farm.* Them two fields was meant to belong together, it'd be a pity if they didn't."

" But you had no pity for the old man," thundered the judge.

" And him going to sell that strip of land to Joudal," stammered the accused.

" So you murdered him for gain."

" No, I never," objected Vondráček indignantly. " It was all along of that field. If them fields had been joined together——"

" Do you plead guilty ? "

" No."

" Then murdering an old man means nothing to you ? "

" But I keep on telling you it was all along of that field," Vondráček burst forth, almost sobbing. " That ain't murder ! Bless my soul, anybody ought to understand that. You see, your honour, it was in the family. I wouldn't do it to a stranger. I've never stolen anything. You ask about Vondráček. And they arrested me like a thief, like a thief," moaned Vondráček, choking with woe.

" No, you're not a thief, but you murdered your father-in-law," said the judge sadly. " Do you know that's punished by death ? "

Vondráček blew his nose and snuffled. " It was all along of that field," he said resignedly ; whereupon the proceedings took their course : evidence, speeches for prosecution and defence.

While the jury retired to discuss the guilt of Vondráček, the judge stared reflectively out of the window.

" Taking it all round, it was a poor show," grumbled the clerk of the court. " The public prosecutor somehow never let himself go properly, and the counsel for the defence hadn't got much to say, either. In fact, it was a clear case, so there was no need to make a lot of talk about it."

The judge snorted. " A clear case," he said with an impatient gesture. " Look here, that man feels just as much in the right as you or I. To my mind it's as if I had to sentence a butcher for slaughtering a cow, or a mole for making mole-hills. I tell you, there were moments when I felt that it wasn't any business of ours at all, you know, not a question of law or justice. Whew ! " he sighed, and took off his robes. " I must have a rest from this for a moment. You know, I think the jury'll let him off. It's absurd, but perhaps they'll let him off, because—— Let me tell you something. I come of peasant stock myself, and when that chap was saying that the fields belong together, well—I saw the two strips of field and I felt that if we had to pass sentence, you know what I mean, by any law of God, then we'd have to pass sentence on those two fields. Do you know what I'd do if I had my way ? I'd stand up, take off my robes and say : Vondráček, in the name of God, because blood that has been shed cries to heaven, you will sow those two fields with henbane ; henbane and thorns ; and until your death you'll have this field of hatred before your eyes. I'd like to know what the public prosecutor would say to that. Sometimes it's God who ought to pass sentence ; He could inflict great and terrible penalties. To pass sentence in God's name—we're hardly equal to that. What, the jury have already made up their minds ? " Sighing with distaste, the judge put on his robes. " Well, come along then. Bring the jury in ! "

The Disappearance of an Actor

*   *   *

IT WAS ON September the second that Benda the actor disappeared—the great Benda, as he had been known ever since, at a leap, he had mounted to one of the highest rungs on the ladder of theatrical fame. Actually, nothing whatever happened on September 2nd ; the charwoman who arrived at nine o'clock in the morning to look after Benda's flat, found the bed disarranged and everything in the state of hopeless disorder which habitually marked Benda's surroundings ; but Benda himself was not at home. As however there was nothing unusual about this, she put the flat straight in her perfunctory manner and proceeded on her way again. Well and good. But from that onwards all trace of Benda was lost.

Mrs. Marešová (that was the charwoman) was not particularly surprised even at that. Actors, you know, are just like gypsies ; nobody can tell where they'll turn up next, either in a theatre or on the spree. But on September 10th there was a regular hue and cry after Benda ; he ought to have come to the theatre where they were beginning to rehearse " King Lear " ; when there were still no signs of Benda at the third rehearsal, they got uneasy and telephoned to Dr. Goldberg, Benda's friend, to find out whether he knew what had become of Benda.

This Dr. Goldberg was a surgeon and earned a fabulous amount of money by removing appendixes ; the Jews go in a lot for that sort of thing. He was a stout man with stout gold glasses and a stout heart of gold, too. He was very keen on art and his flat was crammed with pictures

from floor to ceiling. He fairly doted on Benda, who
treated him with a friendly disdain, and with a certain con-
descension allowed him to pay for his drinks (which, between
ourselves, was no trifle). Benda's tragic countenance and
the beaming face of Dr. Goldberg (who drank nothing but
water) added to the effect of all those tremendous sprees and
mad escapades which represented the seamy side of the
great actor's fame.

So they telephoned to this Dr. Goldberg from the theatre
and asked him what had happened to Benda. He said he
had no idea, but that he'd go and look for him; he did not
say that for a whole week he had been searching for him with
increasing anxiety in all the night clubs and other likely
resorts. He had an uneasy foreboding that something had
happened to Benda. It was like this : As far as could be
ascertained, Dr. Goldberg was the last to have seen Jan
Benda. Some time at the end of August he had accompanied
him on a triumphal jaunt through the night-life of Prague ;
but after that, Benda had failed to come to any of their
usual meetings. Perhaps he's ill, said Dr. Goldberg to himself at last, and one evening he proceeded to Benda's flat ;
that had been on the first of September. He rang the bell ;
nobody had opened the door but he could hear some sort of
noise inside. Thereupon Dr. Goldberg had gone on ringing
the bell for a good five minutes ; suddenly he heard the
sound of footsteps and the door opened ; there stood
Benda, wrapped in a dressing-gown and Dr. Goldberg was
aghast at the sight of him, so forbidding did the famous
actor look with his hair tousled and matted, and a full week's
growth of stubble on his face ; also he seemed haggard and
unwashed.

" So it's you, is it ? " he said in a surly tone. " What
do you want ? "

" Good heavens, what's the matter with you ? " burst forth Dr. Goldberg.

" Nothing," snarled Benda. " I'm not going out any-where, if that's what you're after. Leave me alone." And he slammed the door in Goldberg's face.

It was on the next day that he had disappeared.

Dr. Goldberg stared glumly through his thick glasses. There was evidently something amiss. The house-porter of the block of flats where Benda lived informed him that only recently, it may have been between the first and second of September, a car had stopped in front of the house at about three o'clock in the morning. Nobody had got out, but the hooter had been sounded as if a sign were being given to someone in the house. Then someone was heard to leave the house and slam the front door ; after that the car drove away. The porter didn't know what kind of car it was, he hadn't gone to look at it. Give us a chance, sir, a man doesn't get out of bed at three in the morning unless he has to. But from the way the hooter had been sounded it seemed as if the people in the car were in the deuce of a hurry and hadn't a moment to lose.

Mrs. Marešová stated that Mr. Benda hadn't gone out for a whole week (unless perhaps at night), hadn't shaved and probably hadn't washed, either, from the look of him. He had sent out for his meals, drank brandy and sprawled on the sofa ; that was about all. Now that others also were beginning to concern themselves about Benda's disappear-ance, Dr. Goldberg went back to Mrs. Marešová.

" Now, my good woman," he said. " Do you happen to know what clothes Mr. Benda was wearing when he went away ? "

" None," said Mrs. Marešová ; " that's just what worries me. He wasn't wearing anything. I know all his suits, and they're all hanging up in the flat—there ain't even a pair of trousers missing."

" But he couldn't have gone out in his underclothes, could he ? " observed Dr. Goldberg, very much startled.

" He hadn't got no underclothes, neither," declared Mrs. Marešová, " nor no boots, neither. That's the funny part of it, sir. See, I've got every bit of his washing all written down, because I takes it to the laundry ; they've just sent it back clean, and I've sorted the things out and counted them over ; he's got eighteen shirts, there ain't one missing, not even a handkerchief, nor nothing, there ain't. All that's gone is a hand-bag that he always carries with him. If he did go away, then he must have been wearing his birthday suit."

Dr. Goldberg looked very grave. " My good woman," he said, " when you arrived there on the second of September, did you notice any special kind of disorder ? You know what I mean, anything turned upside down or any doors broken open ? "

" Disorder," observed Mrs. Marešová, " there was the same disorder there like what there always is. Mr. Benda, sir, he's an untidy man, if ever there was one. But beyond that, there wasn't no disorder, not to speak of, there wasn't. But where could he have ·gone to when he hadn't got a rag to his body, I· ask you ? "

Dr. Goldberg, however, could no more explain that than she could, and with the gloomiest of misgivings he now applied to the police.

" Right you are," said the police inspector, when Dr. Goldberg had trotted out all he knew. " We'll have a look for him. But from all you've told me about the way he shut himself up at home for a whole week, without washing or shaving and sprawling on the sofa, drinking brandy and then disappearing stark-naked like an African nigger, why, sir, that looks to me like a—hm—well, what you might call a——"

" Fit of insanity," Dr. Goldberg blurted out.

" That's it, sir," said the police-inspector ; " suicide while of unsound mind. You know, I shouldn't be surprised if that's what he has done."

" But then his body would be found," suggested Dr. Goldberg dubiously.

" And besides, how far could he go if he was naked ? And why should he take his bag with him ? And the car that was waiting in front of the house ? That looks more as if he was running away, sir."

The police-inspector remembered something else :

" By the way, was he in debt at all ? "

" No," said the doctor hastily. As a matter of fact Benda was up to his eyes in debts, but he never took them at all seriously.

" Or was there—hm—any private scandal, was he crossed in love, or was he worried about his health or had he got any sort of trouble out of the ordinary ? "

" Not as far as I know," replied Dr. Goldberg hesitatingly ; he did recall one or two things, but he kept them to himself. And anyhow, they could hardly have any bearing upon Benda's inexplicable disappearance. All the same, on his way home from the police—of course, the police would do all they could—he turned over in his mind everything he knew about Benda in that respect. There was not much.

1. Benda had a wife somewhere abroad, but he did not worry himself about her.

2. He was keeping a girl in one of the outlying districts of Prague.

3. He was having what is called an affair with a lady named Greta, the wife of the big industrialist Korbel. Greta was extremely anxious to go on the stage, and for that

reason Mr. Korbel had financed some films in which his wife, of course, played the star parts. It was notorious that Benda was Greta's lover, that Greta followed him about and was no longer showing even a reasonable amount of discretion. As a matter of fact, Benda never talked about these things ; he despised the whole business, which he treated partly with lordly airs and graces, and partly with a cynicism which made Goldberg shudder. No, said the doctor to himself hopelessly, nobody knows all the ins and outs of Benda's private life ; I'll be hanged if this isn't a case of foul play, but that's a matter for the police to deal with.

Dr. Goldberg of course did not know what the police were doing and what was their line of action. With an increasing despondency he kept on waiting for news. Meanwhile a whole month elapsed since the disappearance of Benda, and people were now beginning to refer to him in the past tense.

One evening Dr. Goldberg ran across Lebduška, an old actor, and as they talked of one thing and another, Benda's name naturally cropped up. " My word, he was an actor and no mistake," remarked old Lebduška. " I remember him when he was about twenty-five years old. It was something terrific, the way he played Oswald in Ibsen's ' Ghosts.' Why, medical students used to go to the theatre to study the symptoms of paralysis ! And then he had a go at King Lear. Well, I can't tell you what he made of the part because my eyes were fixed on his hands the whole time. He had hands like an old man of eighty, all skinny and shrivelled up, pitiful hands they were, and to this day I can't make out how he managed it. I know a thing or two about make-up, myself, but nobody's ever been a patch on Benda for that sort of thing. And it takes an actor to realize what a job like that amounts to."

It caused Dr. Goldberg a melancholy pleasure to listen to this obituary notice of Benda by a fellow-actor.

" He took his acting seriously, he did," sighed Lebduška. " The way he used to bully the theatrical wardrobe master ! *I won't play the king*, he'd shout, *if you shove such shoddy lace on my coat !* And he wouldn't let himself be fobbed off with any fake property stuff. Why, when he was going to play Othello, he went round to all the old curiosity shops, if you please, till he found an old Renaissance ring ; and that's what he wore when he played Othello. He said he could act better when he had the real thing on him like that. The way he played a part, you couldn't call it acting, it was nothing less than— incarnation," said Lebduška hesitantly, not knowing whether he were using the right word or not. " And when he was in a show, during the intervals, he was as grumpy as a bear with a sore head and he'd lock himself up in his dressing-room, so that nobody could interfere with the mood he was in. That's why he drank so much that it wrecked his nerves," remarked Lebduška reflectively. " Well, I'm going into this cinema," he added, by way of a parting remark.

" I'll come with you," suggested Dr. Goldberg, who was at a loose end that evening. They were showing a naval film there, but Dr. Goldberg had no very clear idea of what it was all about. Almost with tears in his eyes he listened to old Lebduška prating about Benda.

" He wasn't an actor," said Lebduška, " he was the very devil. One life wasn't enough for him, and that's all about it. He was a bit of a bounder in his private life, but on the stage he was a king from head to foot or he was a vagabond from head to foot. I tell you, he used to wave his hand as if he'd been ruling the roost all his life, and yet his father was nothing more or less than a knife-grinder who used to pad the hoof. I say, look at that chap who's supposed to be shipwrecked ; he's on a desert island and his nails have been manicured. What a damned fool. And do you see the way he's got a beard just stuck on his face ? If Benda had been playing that part, he'd have let a real beard grow and he'd have had some real dirt under his nails. Here, I say, doctor, what's come over you all of a sudden ? "

" Excuse me," stammered Dr. Goldberg, standing up. " But I've just thought of something. Thanks very much." And he was already dashing out of the cinema. Benda would have let a real beard grow, he repeated. Benda *did* let a real beard grow ! Why on earth didn't I think of that before ?

" To police headquarters ! " he shouted as he flung himself into the nearest taxi, and when he got as far as the sergeant who was on night duty, he begged and prayed of him for heaven's sake to find out immediately, but it must be *immediately*, whether on September the second or thereabouts they had discovered the body of an unknown tramp —yes, no matter where. Contrary to all expectation the sergeant did actually go off to look the matter up or to inquire about it, probably more from sheer boredom than from any actual zeal or interest ; meanwhile Dr. Goldberg was on tenterhooks, for a horrible idea had dawned upon him.

" Well, sir," said the sergeant when he returned, " on the morning of September the second a gamekeeper found the body of an unknown tramp about forty years old in the woods at Křivoklát ; on September the second the body of an unknown man was taken out of the Elbe near Litoměřice —he was about thirty and had been in the water for at least a fortnight ; on September the tenth an unknown man, of about sixty, hanged himself near Německý Brod——"

" Are there any particulars known about that tramp ? " asked Dr. Goldberg breathlessly.

" Murder," said the sergeant, gazing attentively at the agitated doctor. " According to the report from the local police-station his skull had been smashed by a blunt instrument. The findings of the post-mortem were : signs of alcoholism ; cause of death, brain injuries. Here's the photograph," said the sergeant and added, with the air of an expert, " My word, he was properly done in and no mistake."

The photograph showed the body only as far as the waist ; it was dressed in verminous rags, with an open calico shirt ; at the place where the forehead and eyes should have been was a ghastly cluster of matted hair and something which perhaps consisted of skin or bones ; only the bristly chin with its growth of stubble and the half-opened mouth bore any resemblance to a human being. Dr. Goldberg trembled like a leaf. Is it—could it possibly be Benda ?

" Had he . . . had he got any special distinguishing marks ? " he managed to inquire in a choked voice.

The sergeant looked into a mass of papers. " Hm, height, five feet eight, hair turning grey, teeth extremely decayed——"

Dr. Goldberg uttered a loud sigh of relief. " That's not him. Excuse me for troubling you," he babbled joyfully, " but that can't be him. Absolutely impossible."

Absolutely impossible, he said to himself with relief, as he returned home. He may still be alive. Perhaps, by Jove, perhaps he's hanging about in some night-club, like Olympia or Black Katie's.

That night Dr. Goldberg had another jaunt through the night-life of Prague ; he drank his glass of water in all the resorts where Benda had once held sway and through his gold goggles he peered into every nook and corner, but there was no sign of Benda anywhere. Towards morning Dr. Goldberg suddenly turned pale, told himself aloud that he was an imbecile and rushed off to his garage.

Early that same morning he had reached the police head-quarters of a certain district and had the chief of police fetched from his bed. Luckily it turned out that with his own hands he had once opened up this gentleman's inside and sewn him together again, on which occasion he had handed him, as a keepsake, an appendix preserved in alcohol. As a result of this by no means superficial acquaintance he secured an exhumation order within two hours, and side by side with a very disgruntled divisional surgeon he was looking on while the corpse of the unknown tramp was being dug up.

"You can take my word for it," growled the divisional surgeon "that the Prague police asked about this fellow before. He can't possibly be Benda. Why, he was a filthy rascal."

"Was there any vermin on him?" asked Dr. Goldberg with interest.

"I don't know," said the divisional surgeon disgustedly, "and now it's not likely that you can recognize anything of him. Hang it all, he's been in the ground for a whole month."

When the grave was opened, Dr. Goldberg had to send for some brandy, otherwise he could not have induced the grave-diggers to lift up and carry into the mortuary the unspeakable object which had been lying at the bottom of the grave, sewn up in a sack.

"You can go and have a look at it yourself," the divisional surgeon snarled at Dr. Goldberg, and he remained in front of the mortuary, smoking a strong cheroot.

After a while Dr. Goldberg staggered out of the mortuary, as pale as death. "Come and look" he gasped, returned to the body and pointed to the place where the man's head had once been. Dr. Goldberg then took his forceps and pulled back what had once been lips; this revealed the repulsively decayed teeth, or rather just the yellow stumps of teeth, stained with black caries. " Have a good look," muttered Goldberg, as he thrust the forceps between the teeth and removed a coating of black decay from them. Underneath it two strong, shining molars became visible. But Dr. Goldberg could stand it no longer. He rushed out of the mortuary, clutching his head in his hands.

When after a while he returned to the divisional surgeon, he was pale and woebegone. " So much for those remarkably decayed teeth," he said softly ;   " that was only a black composition that actors put on their teeth when they are playing the parts of very old men or tramps. That filthy rascal was an actor, and," he added, with a despairing gesture of the hand, " a very great actor, too."

The same day Dr. Goldberg called on the industrialist Korbel ; he was a tall, powerful man with a chin like a battering-ram and a body like a buttress.

" I have come to see you," said Dr. Goldberg, gazing fixedly at him through his convex glasses " in connexion with Benda, the actor."

" Oh ! " said the manufacturer, and joined his hands behind his head, " has he turned up again ? "

" Partly," remarked Dr. Goldberg ; " and I think it'll interest you . . . if for no other reason, on account of the film that you were going to produce, or rather finance, with him in it."

" On account of what film ? " asked the great man with an air of boredom, " I know nothing about it."

" I mean," said Goldberg obdurately, " the film in which Benda was to have played the part of a tramp, with your wife as leading lady. As a matter of fact, it was to have been produced because of your wife," added the doctor guilelessly.

" That's nothing to do with you," snarled Korbel. " I suppose that Benda came to you with some story or other. That was all premature talk. There may have been a plan of some sort in the air. Benda told you that, didn't he ? "

" Not a bit of it ! You yourself gave him strict orders not to breathe a word about it to a soul. You made a regular mystery of it. But you know that during the last week of his life Benda let his beard and hair grow to make him look like a tramp. He used to make a very thorough job of details like that, didn't he ? "

" I don't know," snapped the factory owner. " Is there anything else you want ? "

" So this film was to have been produced on September the second, wasn't it ? The first scene was to be taken in the woods at Křivoklát at daybreak ; the tramp wakes up on the edge of a clearing in the morning mist and shakes the leaves and pine-cones from his rags. I can just imagine how Benda would have played that. I'm sure he put on the shabbiest rags and footwear he'd got ; he had a packing-case filled with them in the attic. That's why, after his . . . disappearance, not a scrap of his linen or clothing was missing—by Jove, fancy nobody thinking of that. It was only to be expected that he'd rig himself out with the sleeves all worn away and a rope round his waist, like a real tramp. It was a hobby of his to pay strict attention to his get-up."

" And what happened then ? " asked the great man, and bent his head farther towards the shadow. " I don't quite know, though, why you're telling me all this."

" Because on September the second at about three o'clock in the morning," continued Dr. Goldberg stubbornly, " you came to fetch him—most probably in a hired car and certainly in a closed one. I expect it was driven by your brother who's a sportsman and keeps his mouth shut. As you'd arranged with Benda beforehand, you didn't go upstairs, but just sounded the hooter below. After a while you were joined by Benda, or rather, by a dirty, scrubby tramp. *Hurry up*, you said to him, *the operator has gone on in advance.* And you drove to the woods at Křivoklát."

" You don't seem to know the number of the car," said the man in the shadow, ironically.

" If I knew it, I'd have had you arrested before this," said Dr. Goldberg in very distinct tones. " At daybreak you were on the spot ; it's a sort of clearing, or, rather, a glade flanked by a row of very old oak trees, a beautiful setting. I rather fancy that your brother stayed with the car on the high-road and pretended to be repairing the engine. You took Benda four hundred paces from the road and there you said to him : *Well, this is the place.* And Benda said, as the idea suddenly occurred to him : *Where's the operator ?* At that instant you struck him the first blow."

" What with ? " inquired the man in the shadow.

" A life-preserver made of lead," said Dr. Goldberg, " because a spanner would have been too light for a skull like Benda's, and what you wanted to do was to smash it to pieces, beyond recognition. When you had finished battering him, you went back to the car. *Ready ?* asked your brother, but you probably didn't say anything, because after all, murdering a man is no trifle."

" You're crazy," bawled the man in the shadow.

" No, I'm not. I just wanted to remind you of how it probably happened. You wanted to get rid of Benda on account of the scandal with your wife. Your wife was carrying on very publicly——"

" You filthy Jew," bellowed the man in the armchair, " how dare you——"

" I'm not afraid of you," said Dr. Goldberg, adjusting his spectacles to give himself a sterner appearance. " You won't get at me, for all your wealth. What harm could you

H

do me ? You might refuse to let me remove your appendix, but I wouldn't advise you to do that."

The man in the shadow burst into quiet laughter. " Look here, my good fellow," he said with a certain cheerfulness, " if you knew for certain only a tenth of what you've just been jabbering to me, you wouldn't come to me, you'd go to the police, wouldn't you ? "

" That's just it," said Dr. Goldberg ruefully. " If I could prove only a tenth of it, I wouldn't be here. I don't suppose it'll ever be proved—not even that the filthy tramp was Benda. That's the very reason I came here."

" To threaten me, eh ? " the man in the arm-chair rapped out and moved his hand towards the electric bell.

" No, but to scare you. It's not likely that you've got a very tender conscience—you're too rich for that. But what will upset your lordly composure till your dying day will be the certainty that somebody else has discovered the whole dastardly business, that somebody knows that you're a murderer, that your brother's a murderer, that you pair of magnates murdered Benda, the actor, the knife-grinder's son, the mummer. As long as you're alive, the pair of you will never have any peace of mind. I'd like to see you on the gallows, but the least I can do as long as I'm alive is to be a nuisance to you. Benda was a bad egg. I know better than anybody how bad, conceited, cynical, impudent and so forth, he was. But he was an artist. All your millions won't make up for that drunken mummer ; with all your millions you'll never manage his high and mighty wave of the hand, the man's sham and yet terrific greatness." Dr. Goldberg threw his hands up despairingly. " How could you do it ? You'll never have any peace of mind, I won't let you forget. Till your dying day I'll keep on reminding you : *Remember Benda the actor. I tell you, he was an artist, if ever there was one*".

An Attempt at Murder

★ ★ ★

THAT EVENING Mr. Tomsa, a higher civil servant, was just relishing his ear-phones, and with a bland smile was listening in on the wireless to a pleasant rendering of Dvořák's dances—that's something like a tune, he said to himself contentedly—when all of a sudden there were a couple of loud reports from outside and glass was scattered with a crash from the window above his head. (The room in which Mr. Tomsa was sitting was on the ground-floor.)

And then he did what any of us would do : first of all, he waited for a moment, to see what was going to happen next, and then, and not till then, he took fright; for he saw that somebody had fired twice at him through the window by which he was sitting. There, opposite him in the doorway, a splinter had been ripped away and beneath it a bullet was embedded. His first impulse was to rush out into the street and with his bare hands to seize the ruffian by the collar. But when a man is getting on in years and has a certain dignity to keep up, he generally gives a first impulse the miss, and decides in favour of the second one. And that is why Mr. Tomsa made a dash for the telephone and rang up the police :

" Hallo ! " he shouted. " Send someone here at once, an attempt has just been made to murder me."

" Where is it ? " said a sleepy and listless voice.

" Here, in my flat." Mr. Tomsa flared up in sudden anger, as if the police could help it. " It's perfectly outrageous to start shooting like this, for no reason at all, at a law-abiding citizen, who's sitting quietly at home. This has got to be looked into very strictly. It's a fine state of affairs when——"

113

" All right," the sleepy voice interrupted him. " I'll send someone to you."

Mr. Tomsa fumed with impatience. It seemed to him an eternity before this someone made his appearance, but in reality only twenty minutes elapsed before a stolid police-inspector had reached him and was examining with interest the window through which the shots had passed.

" Someone's been shooting here, sir," he said soberly.

" I could have told you that," burst forth Mr. Tomsa. " Why, I was sitting here by the window."

" Seven millimetres calibre," announced the inspector, extricating the bullet from the door by means of a knife. " Looks as if it's been fired from an old army revolver. Just look here. The chap, whoever he was, must have been standing on the fence. If he'd been standing on the pavement the bullet would have gone in higher up. That means he must have been aiming at you, sir."

" That's funny," observed Mr. Tomsa bitterly. " I almost thought he was trying to hit the door."

" And who did it ? " asked the inspector, ignoring this interruption.

" I'm sorry I can't give you his address," said Mr. Tomsa. " I didn't see the gentleman and I forgot to invite him inside."

" That makes things difficult," remarked the inspector placidly. " And who do you suspect ? "

Mr. Tomsa's supply of patience gave out.

" Suspect ? " he began irritably. " Man alive, I never saw the blackguard, and even if he'd been good enough to wait till I'd blown a kiss to him through the window, I couldn't have recognized him in the darkness. My dear sir, if I knew who it was, do you think I'd have bothered you to come here ? "

" Well, yes, there's something in that, sir," replied the

inspector soothingly. " But perhaps you can think of somebody who'd profit by your death, or who might want to pay
you out for something. . . . You see, sir, this wasn't no
attempted burglary. A burglar don't shoot unless he has
to. But there may be somebody who's got a grudge against
you. That's for you to say, sir, and then we'll look into it."

Mr. Tomsa was taken aback. He hadn't thought of it in
that light.

" I haven't the faintest idea," he said waveringly, casting
a glance over the peaceful life he had led as a civil servant
and a bachelor. " Who could have a grudge against me ? "
he said in bewilderment. " As far as I know, I haven't a
single enemy in the world, most positively I haven't. The
thing's quite impossible," he added, shaking his head.
" Why, I never fall out with anyone ; I keep entirely to
myself. I never go anywhere, I never poke my nose into
anything. What should anyone want to pay me out for ? "

The inspector shrugged his shoulders.

" I don't know, sir. But perhaps you'll think of something by to-morrow. You won't be nervous here by yourself ? "

" No," said Mr. Tomsa in a reflective tone. It's queer,
he said to himself uneasily when he was alone ; why anybody
should shoot at me, at me of all people. Why, I'm almost
a hermit. I attend to my work in the office and I go home
—why, I scarcely ever come into contact with anyone.
Why should they want to shoot me, then ? he wondered
with increasing bitterness at such ungracious behaviour ;
little by little he began to pity himself. Here I've been
slaving away like a horse, he said to himself, even taking
work home with me, never extravagant, never giving myself
a treat, living like a snail in its shell, and bang ! someone
comes along to put a bullet into me. My goodness, it's
queer how fiendish people are, marvelled Mr. Tomsa aghast.

What have I ever done to anyone ? Why should anyone have such a shocking, such an insane hatred for me ?

Perhaps there's some mistake, he began to reassure himself, as he sat on the bed, holding the boot he had taken off. The man just took me for somebody else he had a grudge against. That must be it, he said to himself with relief, because why, why should anyone hate me like that ?

The boot fell from Mr. Tomsa's hand. Well, of course, he suddenly reminded himself with a slight sense of embarrassment, that was a silly thing for me to do, but it was really nothing but a slip of the tongue ; I was talking to Roubal and, without meaning to, I made a nasty remark about his wife. Of course, everyone knows the minx carries on with Tom, Dick, and Harry, and he knows it too, but he doesn't want to let people see he does. And I, ass that I was, went and stupidly blurted it out. . . . Mr. Tomsa remembered how Roubal had merely gulped and dug his nails into his clenched hands. Good heavens, he said to himself horrified, the man was cut to the quick. Why, he must be madly in love with her. Of course, I tried to smooth matters over, but my word, didn't he bite his lips ! There's no doubt he's got good reason for hating me, reflected Mr. Tomsa gloomily. I know he didn't shoot at me, that's nonsense, but I really couldn't be surprised if——

Mr. Tomsa stared at the floor abashed. Or what about that tailor, he reminded himself, very constrainedly. For fifteen years I used to order my clothes from him and then one day I was told that he was in the last stage of consumption. Of course, a man fights shy of wearing clothes that a consumptive tailor has been coughing into, so I stopped getting my suits from him. And then he came and begged and prayed of me, saying he hadn't got a stitch of work to do, that his wife was ill and that he wanted to send his children away ; if I'd only let him have the pleasure of my custom again. Good heavens, the poor fellow looked as pale as a ghost and from the way he sweated I could see how ill he was. Mr. Kolinsky, I said to him, look here, it's no use, I need a better tailor ; you haven't given me satisfaction. I'll try my hardest, sir, he stammered, sweating with fright and shame ; it's a wonder he didn't burst out crying. And I, Mr. Tomsa reminded himself, I just sent him away saying " I'll see," the sort of remark that poor devils like that know only too well. There's a man who might hate me, said Mr. Tomsa to himself in alarm ; it must be an awful thing to go and beg and pray of someone for your very life and to be sent away so unfeelingly. But what was I to do with him ? I know he couldn't have done it, but——

Mr. Tomsa began to feel more and more downhearted. That was another unpleasant business, he reminded himself, the way I gave our office messenger a wigging. There was a file I couldn't find and so I sent for the old fellow and called him names as if he'd been a schoolboy, and in front of other people, too. This is what you call keeping things in order, I suppose, you idiot, you make the whole place look like a pig-sty ; I ought to give you the sack. And then I found the file in my own drawer. And the poor old chap never murmured, he just trembled and blinked his eyes. A surge of heat caused Mr. Tomsa to wince. A man can't very well apologize to an underling, he said to himself peevishly, even if he has been a little hard on him. But how those subordinates must hate their seniors. Wait a bit, I'll give the old fellow some cast-off clothes ; but perhaps that would be humiliating for him, too.

Mr. Tomsa now found it unbearable to continue lying in bed ; the counterpane was stifling him. He sat on the bed with his arms round his knees and stared into the darkness. Then there was that affair with young Morávek in the office, he reflected with a pang. He's a well-educated fellow and writes poems. And when he made a blunder in dealing with those papers, I said to him : *Do it all over again, young man,* and I meant to throw the papers on to the table, but they fell under his feet, and when he bent down to pick them up he was quite red, his eyes were red. I could have kicked myself, growled Mr. Tomsa. Why, I'm quite fond of the young fellow, and then to go and humiliate him like that, even without intending to.

Another face floated into Mr. Tomsa's mind, the pale and hollow face of his colleague, Wankl. Poor Wankl, he said to himself, he wanted to be clerk in charge, and I was appointed instead. It would have meant a few hundred crowns more every year and he's got six children. I heard that he wanted to have his eldest daughter trained as a singer, but he can't afford it, and I was promoted above his head because he's such a slow-witted duffer and a drudge. His wife's bad-tempered, terribly skinny and bad-tempered through having to be always pinching and scraping ; he swallows a dry roll for his midday lunch—Mr. Tomsa lapsed into dismal thoughts. Poor Wankl, he must feel down in the mouth when he sees me without any family, getting a bigger salary than he has ; but how can I help it ? I always feel rather uncomfortable when he looks at me in that surly and reproachful way he's got.

Mr. Tomsa rubbed his forehead, on which the sweat of anguish had broken out. Yes, he said to himself, and then there was a waiter who did me out of a few crowns ; and I sent for the proprietor and he dismissed the waiter on the spot. You thief, he snarled at him, I'll see that nobody in Prague gives you a job. And the man never said a word, but just went away ; I could see his shoulder-blades sticking out under his jacket.

Mr. Tomsa now found his bed unbearable ; he sat down by his wireless set and put on the head-phones ; but the wireless set was silent, amid the silent night, the silent hours of the night ; and Mr. Tomsa covered his face with his hands and recalled all the people he had ever met, the queer and paltry people whom he hadn't got on with and had forgotten about.

In the morning he called at the police-station ; he was rather pale and ill at ease. " Well, sir," asked the police inspector, " have you thought of anyone who's likely to have a grudge against you ? "

Mr. Tomsa shook his head. " I don't know," he said hesitantly. " You see, there's so many who are likely to have a grudge against me that——" He made a helpless gesture with his hand. " The fact of the matter is you never can tell how many people you may have done harm to. You know, I'm not going to sit by that window any more. And I've come to ask you to drop the whole matter."

Discharged

★　　★　　★

"WELL, ZARUBA, do you understand?" asked the prison governor when, in an almost solemn tone, he had finished reading the appropriate document from the Ministry of Justice. "That means that the remainder of your sentence is conditionally remitted. You have served twelve and a half years, and throughout that period your conduct has been—hm—exemplary; we have given you the best of testimonials, and—er—in a word, you can now go home, do you understand? But remember, Záruba, if you should get up to any mischief, the conditional discharge will be withdrawn and you'll have to serve the full life sentence for having murdered your wife Marie, and once that happens, nothing on earth can save you. So take great care, Záruba; the next time it'll be till you die."

The governor blew his nose with emotion.

"You've been a favourite with us here, Záruba, but I don't want to see you here any more. Well, good-bye, and the superintendent will pay you your money. You may go."

Záruba, a lanky fellow, more than six feet in height, shuffled to and fro, and stammered something or other; he was so happy that it hurt, and something gurgled inside him as if he were about to start sobbing.

"Come, come," said the governor gruffly. "Don't start weeping here. We've got some clothes ready for you, and Mr. Málek, the builder, has promised me that he'll take you on. What's that, you want to have a look at your home first? Aha! At your wife's grave. Well, well, that's very decent of you. And now, Mr. Záruba, the best of luck," said the governor hastily and shook hands with Záruba. " And for goodness' sake, take care what you do ; remember we've only let you out conditionally."

" Quite a decent chap," said the governor, as soon as the door had closed behind Záruba. " I tell you, Formánek, these murderers are nearly always nice fellows ; the worst of the lot are the embezzlers, they're never satisfied with anything in jail. I'm sorry for that chap, Záruba."

When Záruba had left behind him the iron gates and the courtyard of Pankrác Prison, he had an uneasy and humble feeling that the nearest warder would stop him and bring him back ; he therefore dawdled a little so as not to make it look as if he were running away. When he got into the street, his head was in a whirl, there were so many people out there, children were scurrying along, two cabmen were having a row, good heavens, what a lot of people, there never used to be so many as that ; which way was he to go ?

It didn't really matter ; nothing but cars, and what a lot of women ; is nobody following me ? No, but what lots of cars there are. Záruba stepped out on the road leading down to Prague, to get away as fast as he could ; the tempting smell of a ham and beef shop was wafted towards him, but not now, not yet ; then there was something with an even stronger smell—some houses being built. The bricklayer Záruba stopped and sniffed the fragrance of mortar and rafters. He watched an old fellow mixing the lime ; he hankered after a little chat, but somehow he could not bring himself to the point, his voice refused to make itself heard ; after a spell of solitary confinement a man gets out of the habit of talking.

Záruba strode down towards Prague. Good heavens, what a lot of buildings ! Here they're doing them all in concrete, twelve years ago it wasn't like that, no, it wasn't like that in my time, thought Záruba, but that's bound to fall down, with thin uprights like that.

" Look out, man, are you blind or what ? "

He nearly got run over by a car, he nearly slipped under a clattering tram ; my goodness, in twelve years a man gets unaccustomed to the streets. He would have liked to ask somebody what that big building was ; he would have liked to ask how to get to the North-Western Railway Station ; as a lorry filled with iron was just rattling past him, he tried to say to himself aloud : " Excuse me, but which is the way to the North-Western Railway Station ? " No, he couldn't manage it ; his voice seemed to have dried up inside him ; up yonder a man gets rusty and dumb ; for the first three years he can still ask a question now and then. " Excuse me, but which is the way——? " was all that he could throatily gasp, but it was not a human voice.

Záruba strode along into the streets. He felt as if he were drunk or as if he were walking in his sleep ; all this is quite different from what it was twelve years ago, bigger, noisier, more confusing. Why, what lots of people ! It made Záruba unhappy, he felt as if he had been somewhere in a foreign country and that he could not even make himself understood to these people. If only he were to get to the station and take the train home . . . His brother had a cottage there, and children . . . " Excuse me, but which is the way—— ?"

Záruba tried to utter the words, but his lips moved soundlessly. Oh well, that'll pass off when I'm home, I'll get into the way of speaking when I'm home ; if only I could get to the railway station. Suddenly there was a shout behind him and someone pushed him on to the pavement. " Man alive, why don't you walk on the pavement ? " a chauffeur snarled at him. Záruba would have liked to answer back, but he couldn't manage it ; he just made a gurgling noise and hurried on. On the pavement, he thought to himself, the pavement's too small for me ; look here, everyone, I'm in such a hurry, I want to get home, excuse me, but which is the way to the North-Western Railway Station ?

I expect this very busy street leads to it, he decided, where all those trams are. Where do all these people come from ? Why, there's crowds and crowds of them and they're all going in one direction—of course, they must be on their way to the railway station, and they're hurrying like that because they don't want to lose the train. The lanky Záruba put his best foot forward so as not to get left behind ; and look now, the pavements are not big enough for the people either, they stream along all over the street, a dense and noisy throng ; and fresh streams of people keep joining them; they are fairly galloping along now and shouting something ; and now they're all beginning to utter a long and ample yell.

Záruba's head was in a whirl with an intoxication of noise. Good heavens, that's fine, such lots of people ! There in the front they were beginning to sing some marching-tune ; Záruba got into step with the others and blithely trudged forward ; hallo, now they're all singing round him. Something thawed and welled up in Záruba's throat, as if it were thrusting itself against him and squeezing its way out, and it was a tune, left right, left right, Záruba was singing a song without words, he growled and grunted to himself in a deep bass voice, what song is this ?

Never mind, I'm going home, I'm going home ! The tall Záruba was now trudging along in the front row and singing ; there were no words to it, but it was fine all the same, left right, left right ; with upraised hands Záruba was trumpeting like an elephant, he felt as if his whole body was full of sound, his entrails quivering like a drum, his chest loudly rumbling and in his throat he felt such enjoyment, such enjoyment as if he were drinking or weeping. Thousands of people were yelling : " Down with the government ! " but Záruba had no idea of what they were calling out, and he exultingly went on trumpeting forth : " Ah-h ! Ah-h ! "

Waving his long arms, Záruba marched at the head of them all, braying and bellowing, singing and raving, drumming on his chest with his fists and uttering a vast yell which towered above the heads of all like a waving banner.

" Uavah, uavah ! " Záruba trumpeted, straining his throat, his lungs, his heart to the utmost, and closing his eyes the while like a crowing cock. " Uavah ! Ah ! Hurrah ! " Now the crowd came to a standstill, and unable to move on, swerved back in a confused coil, panting and scuffling as they shouted with excitement. " Uavah ! Hurrah ! "

Záruba with closed eyes was surrendering to this vast and liberated voice which arose from within him. Suddenly, hands clutched at him and the voice of someone out of breath gasped into his ear : " In the name of the law I arrest you ! "

Záruba opened his eyes as wide as he could ; a policeman was clinging to one of his arms and dragging him out of the crowd which swayed convulsively to and fro. Záruba moaned with terror and tried to wrench his arm from the grasp of the policeman who was twisting it ; Záruba thereupon yelled with pain and, using his other hand like a mallet, he hit the policeman on the head. The policeman's face flushed and he let go ; then Záruba's head was struck by a truncheon and again and again and again. Two huge arms revolved like the sails of a windmill and descended on a number of heads ; at this point two people in helmets, like bulldogs, clutched the huge arms; Záruba, muttering with fear, tried to shake them off, kicking and struggling like mad ; he was lugged and thrust forward, two policemen frog-marched him along the empty street, left right, left right. Záruba went like a lamb ; excuse me, which is the way to the North-Western Railway Station ? I've got to go home.

The two policemen nearly flung him head first into the charge-room.

" What's your name ? " a cold and surly voice snapped at him.

Záruba wanted to speak, but all he could do was to move his lips.

" Come along, what's your name ? " bellowed the surly voice.

" Antonin Záruba," whispered the lanky fellow in sibilant tones.

" Where do you live ? "

Záruba shrugged his shoulders helplessly. " In Pankrác Prison," he managed to articulate. " Solitary confinement."

Of course, it shouldn't have been done, but it was ; three lawyers—the president of the senate, the public prosecutor and the defending counsel attached to the court—discussed how they could get Záruba out of it.

" If you ask me, Záruba had better deny all knowledge of the matter," remarked the public prosecutor.

" That's no good," grunted the president of the senate. " When he was had up, he admitted having assaulted the police. The blithering idiot, now he's admitted——"

" If the policemen," suggested the defending counsel " were to give evidence to the effect that they can't identify Záruba with absolute certainty, that it may have been someone else——"

" Look here," protested the public prosecutor, " we can't very well incite the police to give false evidence. Besides, they've definitely identified him. I'm in favour of unfitness to plead. Suggest a remand for the state of his mind to be inquired into. I'll back you up."

" That's all very well," said the defending counsel, " I'll suggest it ; but suppose the doctors say he isn't mad.".

" I'll talk to them," volunteered the president of the senate. " It's not quite regular, but—— Damn it all ! I shouldn't like to see this fellow Záruba spend the rest of his life in prison just because he acted the fool. Anything but that. Good Lord, I'd give him six months without moving an eyelid ; but I can't stomach the idea of him spending the rest of his life in prison afterwards, I'm hanged if I can."

" If unfitness to plead can't do the trick," remarked the public prosecutor, " it's a deuced poor look-out for him. Confound it all, I've got to take action against this and treat it as a criminal offence. How else can I deal with it ? If the fool had only been in a pub at the time, we could have made out that he wasn't responsible for his actions or something of that sort——"

" Well, gentlemen, you must arrange matters for me somehow," urged the president of the senate, " so that I can discharge him. At my age I wouldn't like to have the responsibility of—well, you know what I mean."

" It's a hard case," sighed the public prosecutor. " Well, we'll see. At any rate the mental experts will keep things going for a bit. The trial's to-morrow, isn't it ? "

But the trial didn't come off. That night Antonin Záruba hanged himself, evidently through fear of the punishment in store for him. On account of his lankiness, he was hanging in a curious posture, as if he were sitting on the ground.

" It's a damned rotten business," growled the public prosecutor. " My word, what a stupid business. But, anyhow, we couldn't help it."

Tales from the other Pocket

★   ★   ★

The Disappearance of Mr. Hirsch

★   ★   ★

"YOU KNOW," began Mr. Taussig, "talking about crimes and so on, you ought to think of your own country first. Hang it all, what do we care what happens in Palermo or wherever it is. But when someone brings off a high-class crime in Prague, why, it sort of flatters my vanity; I say to myself: now we'll be talked about all over the world, and you know, it fairly warms the cockles of my heart. And then too, it stands to reason, when a first-rate crime is committed in any locality, it's good for trade there; it's a sign of prosperity and altogether it arouses confidence. But you've got to collar the criminal.

"I don't know whether you still remember the case of old Hirsch in Long Street; he used to deal in skins, but now and then he also sold Persian carpets and such-like Oriental goods; you know, for several years he was in business in Constantinople, but when he came back from there he had something the matter with his liver; the consequence was, he was as skinny as a dead cat and the colour of something from a tannery. And the carpet-sellers from Armenia or Smyrna used to call on him because he could talk to them in their thieves' lingo. They're awful swindlers, are those Armenians; even a Jew has to be careful with them. Anyway, this fellow Hirsch had his skins on the ground floor, and from there a crooked staircase led to his office; behind the office was where he lived, and that's where Mrs. Hirsch used to sit—she was so fat that she couldn't even walk.

" Now one day towards noon one of the shop-assistants went up to the office to ask Mr. Hirsch whether they were to send any skins on credit to a certain Weil, of Brno ; but Mr. Hirsch was not in the office. This was rather odd, but the shop-assistant thought that probably Mr. Hirsch had gone for a moment into the next room to speak to Mrs. Hirsch. But after a while the maid came from upstairs to say that Mr. Hirsch was to come to lunch. ' How do you mean, to lunch,' said the shop-assistant ; 'why, Mr. Hirsch is at home.' 'How can he be at home,' retorted the maid ' when Mrs. Hirsch has been sitting all day next door to the office and hasn't seen him since the morning ? ' ' And we,' said the shop-assistant, ' haven't seen him either, have we, Václav ? ' (Václav was the errand-boy.) ' At ten o'clock I took the letters in to him,' continued the shop-assistant, ' and Mr. Hirsch told me off because we ought to have written to re-mind Lemberger about those calf-skins ; there were no signs of him after that,' ' My goodness gracious,' said the maid, ' he's not in the office ; perhaps he went out.' ' He didn't go through the shop,' said the shop-assistant ; ' if he had, we'd have seen him, wouldn't we, Václav ?   Perhaps he went through his flat.' ' He can't have,' said the maid, ' or Mrs. Hirsch would have seen him.' ' Well, look here,' said the shop-assistant, ' when I saw him, he was wearing a dressing-gown and slippers ; go and see whether he's taken his boots, goloshes and overcoat '—you know, this was in November and it had been raining quite a lot. ' If he got dressed,' said the shop-assistant, ' he went out somewhere ; if not, he must be at home, mustn't he ? '

" So the maid rushed upstairs and after a while she came back quite flabbergasted. ' My goodness me, Mr. Hugo,' she said to the shop-assistant, ' Mr. Hirsch didn't take his boots or anything ; and Mrs. Hirsch says he couldn't have gone through the flat, because if he had, he'd have had to go through her room.' ' He didn't go through the shop, either,' said the shop-assistant ; ' in fact, he hasn't been in the shop at all to-day, he only called me into the office about the letters. Václav, go and look for him.' So first of all they dashed into the office ; nothing was disarranged there, they only saw a few carpets rolled up in a corner and on the desk was an unfinished letter to Lemberger ; and the gas was still alight above the desk. ' It's quite certain,' said Hugo, ' that Mr. Hirsch hasn't gone anywhere ; if he'd gone anywhere he'd have turned the gas out, wouldn't he ? He must be somewhere in the flat.' So they searched the whole flat, but they found nothing at all. Mrs. Hirsch in her arm-chair began to cry bitterly ; ' it looked,' said this fellow Hugo afterwards, ' as if a large dollop of jelly was shaking to and fro.' ' Mrs. Hirsch,' said Hugo—it's an extraordinary thing how smart these young Jews can be when they're in a tight corner—' Mrs. Hirsch, don't you cry ; Mr. Hirsch can't have run away, because business is brisk just now, and besides, he hasn't been collecting any outstanding debts ; he must be somewhere about. If he doesn't turn up by the evening, we'll tell the police about it, but not before then ; you know, Mrs. Hirsch, if there's any fuss, it isn't good for business.'

" Well, they waited and searched till the evening, but there was no sign of Mr. Hirsch. So when Mr. Hugo had shut the shop at the usual hour, he went to the police station to report that Mr. Hirsch was missing. Detectives were sent and, as you can guess, they ransacked everything, but even then they didn't find the slightest clue ; they looked for blood on the floor, but no, nothing at all ; so, for the time being, they sealed up the office. They then cross-examined Mrs. Hirsch and the staff as to what had happened that morning. But nobody had noticed anything out of the ordinary ; only Mr. Hugo remembered that shortly after nine o'clock a Mr. Lebeda, a commercial traveller, had called on Mr. Hirsch and talked to him for about ten minutes. So they searched for Mr. Lebeda, and, as you can imagine, they discovered him playing poker in the Café Bristol. So Lebeda made a grab at the pool, but the detective said to him : ' We haven't come about your poker-game to-day, Mr. Lebeda, but on account of Mr. Hirsch ; you see, he's missing and you are the last who saw him.' That was right enough, but Lebeda couldn't tell them anything either ; he'd been to see Mr. Hirsch about some straps and hadn't noticed anything out of the way ; only it struck him that Mr. Hirsch was looking seedier than usual. ' You're sort of wasting away, Mr. Hirsch,' he said to him. ' Yes,' said the detective, ' but even supposing Mr. Hirsch was nothing but skin and bone, he couldn't have vanished into thin air, could he ? There'd have been at least some bones or teeth left behind, wouldn't there ? And they couldn't have taken him away in an attaché-case.'

" But as you'll see, the end of the story takes a different turn. You know the cloak-rooms at railway stations, where passengers leave trunks and what not. Well, it was about two days after the disappearance of Mr. Hirsch and the woman in charge of the cloak-room told a porter that she'd got a trunk there and somehow she didn't like the look of it. ' I don't know why it is,' she said, ' but I'm downright scared of that trunk.' So the porter went and sniffed at the trunk and said : ' I'll tell you what, ma, you'd better report this to the railway police.' So they brought along a police-dog and when he'd sniffed at the trunk he began to yelp and his coat went all bristly. That alone made things look a bit fishy, so they prised open the trunk : and inside it there was the corpse of Mr. Hirsch in his dressing-gown and slippers, all

hunched together.   And on account of him having something
the matter with his liver, the poor old chap was already
noticeable, like.   And there was some strong twine cutting
into his neck ; he'd been strangled.   But the funny part of
it was how in his dressing-gown and slippers he could have
got from his office into the trunk at the railway-station.

" It was Superintendent Mejzlik who was put in charge
of the case.   He had a look at the corpse and saw at once
that on the face and hands there were some green, blue and
red stains ; what made them all the more striking was that
Mr. Hirsch was so swarthy.   ' That's a funny symptom of
decomposition,' said Mr. Mejzlik to himself and tried to wipe
off one of the stains with his handkerchief ; and sure enough
he got rid of the stains.   ' Upon my word,' he said to the
other detectives, ' this looks to me like some sort of aniline
dye.   I'll have to pay another visit to that office.'

" Well, first of all, he searched the office to see if he could
find any dyes there, but there weren't any ; and all at once
the rolls of Persian carpets caught his eye.   He unrolled one
of them and rubbed the blue pattern on it with a wetted
handkerchief ; it left a blue stain on his handkerchief.
' These carpets are damned trash,' said the superintendent,
and searched some more ; on Mr. Hirsch's table he found
two or three stubs of Turkish cigarettes in the tray of the
inkpot.   ' Now, bear in mind, my dear fellow,' he said to one
of the detectives, ' that when they're doing some business in
Persian carpets, they always keep on smoking cigarettes ;
that's just one of their Oriental customs.'   And then he sent
for Mr. Hugo.   ' Mr. Hugo,' he said to him, ' after Mr.
Lebeda left, there wasn't anyone else here, was there ? '

" ' Yes, there was,' said Mr. Hugo, ' but Mr. Hirsch never
wanted us to mention it.   You look after the skins, he used
to say to us, but the carpets are nothing to do with you ;
they're my business.'

" ' Of course,' said Mr. Mejzlik, ' because they're smuggled carpets ; look here, not one of them has got the customs stamp. If Mr. Hirsch wasn't in a better world, he'd be in a fine old mess with the Inland Revenue and he'd have to pay a devil of a huge fine. Now out with it, quick, who was it ? '

" ' Well,' said Mr. Hugo, ' at about half-past ten there was an Armenian or a Jew of some sort drove up in an open car, a fat, yellow-faced fellow, and he asked in Turkish or some such lingo for Mr. Hirsch. So I showed him the way up to the office. And behind him was a lanky chap, a valet or something, as thin as a rake and as black as your hat, and he carried five big rolls of carpet on his shoulder ; Václav and me couldn't help wondering at the time how he could manage it. Well, the pair of them went into the office and were there for about a quarter of an hour ; we didn't take any particular notice of it, but the whole time we could hear that shyster talking to Mr. Hirsch. Then the valet came downstairs again, but this time he only had four rolls of carpet on his shoulders ; *Aha, I said to myself, so Mr. Hirsch has bought another carpet.* Oh yes, and when the Armenian was in the doorway of the office, he turned round and said something to Mr. Hirsch, who was inside the office, but I couldn't understand what he was saying. And then the lanky chap threw the carpets into the car and off they drove. The only reason I never mentioned it ' said Mr. Hugo, ' was because there was nothing queer about the business, was there ? It was quite common for carpet-dealers like that to pay us a call, and everyone of them's a crook.'

" ' You know, Mr. Hugo,' said Mr. Mejzlik, ' I may as well tell you that there was something queer about the business. What happened was that the lanky chap carried off Mr. Hirsch's body in one of those rolls of carpet, do you see ?

Damn it all, man, you might have noticed that he had more trouble going down than going up.'

" ' That's true enough,' said Hugo, and turned pale ; ' of course, now I come to think of it, he was quite doubled up. But that can't be right, sir ; that fat Armenian was following him and was talking to Mr. Hirsch through the doorway of the office.'

" ' Why, of course,' said Mr. Mejzlik, ' he was just talking to the empty office.   And while the lanky fellow was strangling Mr. Hirsch, the other chap was talking away sixteen to the dozen, wasn't he ?   Ah, Mr. Hugo, those Armenian Jews are one too many for you.   And then they carried the corpse of Mr. Hirsch in that roll of carpet to their hotel ; but as it was raining and the damned carpet had been dyed with aniline, the colour ran and got on to Mr. Hirsch's face. That's as plain as a pikestaff, isn't it ?   And then, in the hotel, they shoved Mr. Hirsch's carcass into a trunk and sent the trunk to the railway station ; and there you are, Mr. Hugo.'

" Now while Mr. Mejzlik was busy with this the secret police had found a clue to the Armenian.   You see, on the trunk was pasted the label of an hotel in Berlin—which proved that the Armenian was in the habit of tipping handsomely ; you know, hotel porters use these labels as international signs to show how much in the way of a tip the owner is good for.   And as this Armenian forked out well, the hotel-porter in Berlin remembered him well ; his name was Mazanian and he was most likely passing through Prague on his way to Vienna ; but they didn't collar him till he'd got as far as Bucharest and there he hanged himself while remanded in custody.   Why he murdered Mr. Hirsch nobody knows ; most likely they had some business disagreement, dating back to the time when Mr. Hirsch was at Constantinople.

" But this affair only shows you," concluded Mr. Taussig reflectively, " that the chief thing in business is to be straight-forward.   If that Armenian had dealt in proper carpets that weren't dyed with cheap aniline, they wouldn't have guessed immediately how Mr. Hirsch was got rid of, would they ? But if people will sell shoddy goods, they'll get paid out for it sooner or later."

The Troubles of a Carpet Fancier

★　　★　　★

"Hm," SAID Dr. Vitásek, "you know, I'm a bit of a connoisseur of Persian carpets ; but I don't mind telling you, Mr. Taussig, that nowadays things aren't what they used to be. Nowadays those swindlers in the Orient won't take the trouble to dye the wool with cochineal, indigo, saffron, camel's wine, gall-nuts and all the rest of the high-class organic dyestuffs ; oh, it's a crying shame. I suppose these Persian carpets are what you might call a lost art now. That's why only the old specimens that were made before 1870 have got any value ; but that's the sort of thing you can only buy when some old family sells their heirlooms ' for family reasons,' as the best people say when they mean ' debts.' Why, I once came across a real Transylvanian carpet in the castle at Rozemberk—one of those tiny praying-carpets that the Turks made in the seventeenth century when they were living in Transylvania : there in this castle the tourists tramp over it in their hobnailed boots and nobody knows how much it's worth—I tell you, it's downright heartbreaking, that it is. And we've got one of the rarest carpets in the world here in Prague, and nobody knows about it.

"Well, it's like this : I know all the carpet-dealers in town and sometimes I have a look around to see what they've got in stock. You see, sometimes the agents in Anatolia and Persia still come across an old specimen which has been stolen from a mosque or somewhere like that, and they wrap it up together with a common-or-garden carpet ; then afterwards the whole bundle is sold by weight, just as it stands.

So I think to myself, supposing they were to wrap up a Ladik or a Bergamo that way ; and I sometimes look in at one of the carpet-dealers, sit down on a pile of carpets, have a smoke and watch them selling Buchara, Saruka and Tabriz carpets to mugs ; and now and then I say, ' What's that you've got underneath, that yellow one ? ' And, by Jove, if it isn't a Hamadan. Well, among my favourite dealers is a certain Mrs. Severyn—she keeps a little shop in a back alley in the Old Town, and sometimes there are some fine Kararams and Kelims to be picked up there. She's a plump, jolly person, who talks nineteen to the dozen and she owns a poodle-bitch so fat that the very sight of it makes you feel sick. It's one of those fat, surly dogs with an asthmatic and cantankerous bark ; I don't like them. Look here, have any of you ever seen a young poodle ? I never have ; if you ask me, all poodles are old, just like all inspectors, auditors and surveyors of taxes are old ; I suppose it's a mark of the breed. But being anxious to keep on good terms with Mrs. Severyn, I always sat in the corner where the bitch Amina was grunting and wheezing on a large carpet folded square-shape and scratched her back ; Amina liked that no end.

" ' Mrs. Severyn,' I said to her one day, ' business must be bad ; why, the carpet I'm sitting on has been here for the last three years.'

" ' It's been here longer than that,' said Mrs. Severyn ; ' it's been folded up in that corner for a good ten years ; but it isn't my carpet.'

" ' Aha,' I said, ' it belongs to Amina.

" ' The idea,' said Mrs. Severyn with a chuckle ; ' it belongs to a lady ; she says she hasn't got enough room for it at home and so she's left it here. It's rather in my way, but anyhow Amina can sleep on it, can't you, Amina ? '

" I just pulled aside the tip of the carpet, although Amina began to growl ferociously. ' Why, this is quite an old carpet,' I said ; ' may I have a look at it ? '

" ' Of course,' said Mrs. Severyn and she took Amina on to her lap. ' Come now, Amina, this gentleman is only going to have a look, and then he'll spread it out again for Amina. Hush, Amina, you mustn't growl. Now then, you silly thing, you.'

" Meanwhile I unrolled the carpet and, I tell you, my heart gave a terrific thump. It was an Anatolian of the seventeenth century, here and there worn threadbare, but, if you know what I mean, it was what they call a ' bird-carpet,' with a pattern of Chintamans and birds ; that, let me tell you, is a sacred and forbidden pattern. You can take my word for it, that it's a great rarity ; and this parti-cular specimen was at least thirty yards square, of a beautiful white colour, interwoven with turquoise blue and cherry pink. . . . I went over to the window, so that Mrs. Severyn couldn't see my face and said : ' That's quite an old bit of stuff, Mrs. Severyn, and here it is lying on your hands and getting absolutely worn out. Look here, you tell that lady that I'll buy it, if she hasn't any room for it.'

" ' That's a bit of a job,' said Mrs. Severyn. ' This carpet isn't for sale, and the lady, she's all the time in places like Merano and Nice. I don't even know when she's home. But I'll try and ask her.'

" ' Yes, please do,' I said with as much indifference as I could, and then went about my business. You know, a collector looks upon it as an affair of honour to pick up a rarity for a song. I know a very rich and important man who collects books ; he doesn't mind giving a few hundreds for some old second-hand book, but he fairly jumps for joy when he picks up the first edition of the poems of Jan Krasoslav Chmelenský for a few pence at a rag-and-bone dealer's. It's just a sport, like stag-hunting. So I had made up my mind that I must get this carpet on the cheap and that then I'd present it to the museum, because that's the only place for a thing of that sort. Only there'd have to be a label on it with an inscription : *Presented by Dr. Vitasek.* After all, everyone's got his private fancies, hasn't he ? But I don't mind admitting that I'd got this one fairly on the brain.

" It was all I could do not to start off on the very next day for this specimen with the Chintamans and the birds ; I could think of nothing else. I must stick it a day longer, I said to myself every day. There are times when we enjoy tormenting ourselves. But after about a fortnight it struck me that somebody else might find that bird-carpet there, and I rushed round to Mrs. Severyn's. ' Well what about it ? ' I gasped from the doorway.

" ' What about what ? ' asked Mrs. Severyn in astonishment, and I collected my thoughts. ' Why,' I said, ' I was just going along the street here and I happened to remember that white carpet. Will the lady sell it ? '

" Mrs. Severyn shook her head. ' It can't be done,' she said, ' she's at Biarritz now and nobody knows when she's coming back.' So I had a look to see whether the carpet was there ; of course, Amina was lying on it, fatter and mangier than ever, and was waiting for me to scratch her on the back.

" Some days later I had to go to London, and once I was there I took the opportunity of calling on Sir Douglas Keith —you know, he's the greatest living authority on Oriental carpets. ' Would you mind telling me,' I said to him, ' the value of a white Anatolian carpet with Chintamans and birds, more than thirty square yards in area ? '

" Sir Douglas looked at me over his spectacles and rapped out almost ferociously : ' None at all.'

" ' How do you mean, none at all,' I said, taken aback. ' Why shouldn't it have any value ? '

" ' Because there's no such carpet that size,' Sir Douglas yelled at me. ' You ought to know perfectly well that the largest carpet with Chintamans and birds that's known is scarcely fifteen square yards.'

" My face went red with joy. ' But supposing,' I said to him, ' that there was a specimen as big as that. What value would it have ? '

" ' None, I tell you,' yelled Sir Douglas. ' A specimen like that would be unique, and how on earth are you going to decide the value of a unique specimen ? If a specimen's unique, it may as easily be worth a thousand pounds as ten thousand pounds. How the dickens do I know ? Anyway, there's no such carpet in existence. Good day, sir.'

" Well, you can just about imagine in what frame of mind I came back. Ye gods, I must get hold of that specimen with Chintamans and birds. That'd be a windfall for the museum. But you must bear in mind that I couldn't very well show that I was so keen on it, because that's not a collector's way. And don't forget that Mrs. Severyn had no particular reason for wanting to sell the tattered old rug that her Amina rolled about on, while the confounded woman who owned the carpet was gadding about from Merano to Ostend and from Baden to Vichy—she must have had a medical dictionary at home with lots of diseases in it. At all events, she was everlastingly in some spa or other. So about every fortnight I used to look in at Mrs. Severyn's to see whether the carpet was still there in the corner with all its birds, I scratched the loathsome Amina till she squealed with delight, and so as not to make it too obvious I bought some sort of carpet each time. I tell you, at home I've got piles and piles of Shiraz, Shirvan, Mossul, Kabristan and other common-or-garden carpets—but among them was a classical Derbent, yes, sir, that you don't see every day, and an old blue Khorasan. But only a collector can understand what I went through for two years. Talk about pangs of love, why, that's nothing to the pangs of a collector ; but the funny thing about it is that no collector has ever been known to commit suicide, though on the contrary, they generally live to a ripe old age ; I suppose it's a healthy sort of passion.

" One day Mrs. Severyn said to me suddenly : ' Well, Mrs. Zanelli that this carpet belongs to was here ; I told her I could find her a customer for that white rug and that anyway it was getting worn out lying here ; but she said it was an heirloom and she didn't want to sell it and I was to leave it where it was.'

" So as you can imagine I went off on my own to find this Mrs. Zanelli. I thought she'd be no end of a society dame, but, as it turned out, she was an ugly old frump with a purple nose and a wig, and her mouth kept giving a queer twitch as far as her left ear.

" ' Madame,' I said, and I couldn't help watching her mouth jerking across her face, ' I'd very much like to buy that white carpet of yours ; of course, it's a bit threadbare, but it'd just be about suitable for—er—my entrance hall.' And as I waited for her to answer, I felt as if my own mouth was beginning to jerk and twitch to the left ; I don't know whether it was catching, or if it was just nervous excitement, but I tell you, I couldn't keep it under.

" ' How dare you ? ' the dreadful woman screeched at me ' Get out of here this very instant, this very instant,' she yelled. ' That's the heirloom my grandfather left. If you won't get out, I'll send for the police. I won't sell any carpets, I'm a von Zanelli, let me tell you. Mary, see this man out of the house.'

" I tell you, I raced down those stairs like a schoolboy. I could have wept with rage and vexation, but what was I to do ? For a whole year after that I kept on looking in at Mrs. Severyn's ; Amina by now had become so fat and bald that she had learnt to grunt. A year later Mrs. Zanelli came back again. It was then that I gave in and did something which as a collector I ought to be ashamed of to my dying day ; I sent a friend of mine to her—Bimbal the solicitor, a smooth-spoken fellow with a beard which always makes women trust him unreservedly—and told him to offer the worthy lady a reasonable sum for that bird carpet. Meanwhile I waited below, as agitated as a suitor who is about to receive his answer. Three hours later Bimbal staggered out of the house, wiping the sweat from his face. ' You blackguard,' he gasped at me, ' I'll wring your neck. I'm damned if I didn't have to listen to the history of the Zanelli family for three whole hours just to oblige you. And let me tell you,' he bawled vindictively, ' you're not going to get that carpet ; seventeen Zanellis would turn in their graves if that heirloom was to get into the museum. My God, what a trick you played me ! ' And with that he took himself off.

" Now you know that when a man gets an idea into his head, he won't let go of it in a hurry ; and if he's a collector, why, he won't stick at murder to get what he wants ; collecting is quite a job for heroes. So I made up my mind that I'd simply steal that carpet with the Chintamans and birds. First of all, I spied out the lay of the land ; Mrs. Severyn's shop is in a courtyard, and at nine o'clock in the evening the passage-way is locked. I didn't want to do any unlocking with a skeleton-key, because that's a job I know nothing about. The passage-way leads to a cellar where anybody could hide before the place is locked. There's also a small shed in the yard, and by getting on to the roof of the shed, you could climb over into the next yard which belongs to a public-house, and you can always get away from a public-house. So it was quite simple ; the only thing was to find a way of opening the shop-window. I bought a glazier's diamond for that job and practised on my own windows, till I knew how to remove a pane of glass.

" Now don't imagine that burglary's a simple matter ; it's harder than performing an operation on the prostate or slicing chunks out of a man's kidneys. In the first place, it's a hard job to avoid being seen. In the second place, it involves lots of waiting and other inconveniences. And in the third place, there's a good deal of uncertainty about it ; you never know what you're likely to run into. Believe me, it's a hard job and a badly paid job. If I found a burglar in my home, I'd take him by the hand and say to him gently : ' Look here, couldn't you manage to rob people in some other way, more convenient to yourself ? '

" I must admit, I don't know how others set about a burgling job, but my own experiences are not exactly encouraging. On the critical evening, as they say, I sneaked into the building and hid on the stairs leading to the cellar. That's how a police report would put it ; what really happened was that for half an hour I loitered about in the rain in front of the doorway, thus becoming conspicuous to all and sundry. At last I made a desperate resolve, just as a man makes a desperate resolve to have a tooth drawn, and went into the passage-way. As a matter of course, I knocked against a servant-girl who had gone to fetch beer in the public-house next door. To soothe her ruffled feelings, I muttered something to the effect that she was a ducky or a darling ; which so scared her that she made her escape. In the meantime I took shelter on the stairs leading to the cellar ; the dirty brutes had got a dustbin standing there with sweepings and other garbage, most of which, while I was engaged upon what I have described as sneaking in, got spilt

with a tremendous clatter. Then the servant-girl came back
with the beer, and told the house-porter with much fluster
that a suspicious character had got into the house. But the
excellent fellow kept cool and remarked that it was probably
someone who was boozed and who had missed his way into
the public-house next door. A quarter of an hour later,
yawning and clearing his throat, he locked the door and
things quietened down. All I could hear was a servant-girl
sobbing loudly somewhere upstairs—it's funny how noisily
servant-girls sob, most likely they fret about something. I
began to feel cold, and besides that, the place smelt sour and
musty ; I groped about, but everything I touched felt somehow slimy. My goodness, what a lot of finger-prints must
have been left there of Dr. Vitásek, our distinguished
specialist for diseases of the urinary organs ! When I
thought it must be midnight, it was only ten o'clock. I
wanted to start my burgling at midnight, but at eleven
o'clock I couldn't stand it any longer and off I went to steal
that carpet. You wouldn't believe what a row you make
when you want to creep along in the dark ; but the people in
that house were sound sleepers. At last I got to the window
and with a fearful scraping began to cut the glass. Inside
there was a muffled bark ; heavens alive, it was Amina.

" ' Amina,' I whispered, ' you ugly brute, keep quiet ;
I've come to scratch your back.' But you know, in the dark,
it's appallingly difficult to coax the diamond into the same
slit as you made at first ; so I fumbled about with the diamond on the pane till at last I pressed a little harder and the
blessed pane snapped right across with a bang. That's the
way, I said to myself, now the whole neighbourhood'll come
dashing up. I'd better see where I can hide ; but nothing
happened. Then with a coolness which was nothing short of
diabolical I got rid of some more panes of glass and opened
the window ; inside, Amina yelped every now and then, but

K

only in a half-hearted sort of way and just as a matter of form, to show that she was doing her duty. So I crawled through the window and made a bee-line for that wretched tyke. ' Amina,' I whispered fervidly, 'where's your back ? Come along now, I'm a friend of yours—you like that, you brute, don't you ? ' Amina writhed with bliss, if a sack can be said to writhe ; and so I said very affably : ' That's right, and now let go, you tyke,' and tried to drag the precious bird carpet away from underneath her. At this point I suppose Amina decided that her property was at stake and began to howl ; she didn't just bark, she fairly set up a howl. ' Come, come Amina,' I hastily remonstrated with her, ' be quiet, you brute ! Wait a moment and I'll spread something better out for you to lie on.' And wallop, I dragged from the wall an ugly, shiny Kirman that Mrs. Severyn thought was the best thing in her shop. ' Amina,' I whispered, ' that's where you're going to bye-bye.' Amina gazed at me with interest ; but scarcely had I stretched out my hand for *her* carpet, than she again set up a howl. I thought they'd hear it miles and miles away. So I again worked the repulsive brute up into a state of ecstasy by a particularly voluptuous process of back-scratching, and took her into my arms ; but the instant I put my hand out to catch hold of that unique white specimen with the Chintamans and birds she snorted asthmatically and began to swear. As true as I'm standing here. ' You brute,' I said at my wits' end, ' I shall have to kill you.'

" Well, you know, this is a thing I can't make out : I looked at that fat, repulsive, vile tyke with the most savage hatred which I have ever felt, but I couldn't kill the brute. I had a good knife, I had a leather belt : I might have cut the animal's throat, or strangled her, but I hadn't the heart. I sat down beside her on that divine carpet and tickled her behind the ears. ' You coward,' I whispered to myself,

' just one movement or two would be enough, and the thing would be done ; you've operated on plenty of people in your time, and you've seen them dying in terror and pain ; why can't you kill a dog ? ' I tell you I gritted my teeth to try to pluck up courage, but I couldn't manage it ; and at that point I broke down and cried—I suppose it must have been because I felt so ashamed of myself. And then Amina began to whine and licked my face.

" ' You wretched, beastly, good-for-nothing freak, you,' I snarled at her, patted her mangy back and climbed through the window into the yard ; I had now reached the stage of defeat and retreat. What I wanted to do next was to jump on to the shed and from there get along the roof to the other yard and out through the pub, but I hadn't an ounce of strength left, or else the roof was higher than I had sup-posed ; at all events I couldn't get on to it. So I climbed back on to the stairs by the cellar and stayed there till morning, absolutely fagged out. Idiot that I was, I might have slept on those carpets, but I never thought of that. In the morning I heard the house-porter opening the door. I waited a moment, and then made straight for the exit. The house-porter was standing in the doorway and when he saw a stranger walking out of the passage he was so flabber-gasted that he forgot to raise an alarm.

" A few days later I called on Mrs. Severyn. A grating had been put in front of the windows, and on the sacred Chintamans design, of course, that disgusting reptile of a dog was coiled up ; when she saw me, she joyously wagged the stumpy sausage which in other dogs would be called a tail. Mrs. Severyn beamed at me. ' That's our darling Amina, our pet, our dear little doggie ; just fancy, the other day a burglar got in here through the window and our Amina chased him away. Why, I wouldn't let her go for all the money in the world,' she declared with pride. ' But she's fond of you ; she can tell an honest person when she sees one, can't you, Amina ? '

" Well, that's the whole story.   That unique white carpet is still lying there—I believe it's one of the rarest specimens of textile-ware in the world ; and still that loathsome, scabby stinking Amina grunts with delight on it.   I wouldn't be surprised if one day she's choked by her own fat, and then perhaps I'll have another try : but first of all I'll have to learn how to file through a grating."

The Stolen Murder

★   ★   ★

" THAT REMINDS me of a case," said Mr. Houdek, " which was very carefully thought out and stage-managed, but I'm afraid you won't care for it, because it's got no proper ending and what was behind it never came out. Anyway, if it bores you, just say so and I'll leave off.

" As you may know, I live in Krucemburk Street at Vinohrady. It's one of those short side-streets without a public-house or a laundress or a grocer's shop, and where the people go to bed at ten o'clock, except the bad lads who stay at home listening to the wireless and don't get to bed until eleven. Most of the people who live there are law-abiding taxpayers or second division civil servants, together with a few fellows who keep goldfish, one man who plays the banjo, two stamp-collectors, one vegetarian, one spiritualist, and one commercial traveller who, as a matter of fact, also goes in for theosophy ; apart from that, all you'll find there are landladies from whom the aforesaid persons rent clean, well-furnished rooms with breakfast, as the advertisements say. Once a week, always on Thursdays, the man who goes in for theosophy doesn't get home till midnight because he's been busy practising with the spirits ; on Tuesdays two of the goldfish experts get home about midnight because they've been to a meeting of the Aquarium League and they stand under a lamp-post arguing about viviparous varieties and telescope fish. Three years ago a drunken man actually passed through the street, but it's supposed that he was from a different neighbourhood and had lost his way. On the other hand, there was a Russian named Kovalenko or Kopytenko who used to come home that way every night at

147

a quarter past eleven. He was a shortish man, with whiskers of a flimsy kind who lived in No. 7, Mrs. Janská's. Nobody knew how this Russian earned his living ; but he used to lounge about at home until five o'clock in the afternoon, then, carrying a portfolio, he went off to catch a tram at the nearest stopping-place and rode to town ; at exactly a quarter past eleven he alighted at the same stopping-place and turned off into Krucemburk Street. Somebody afterwards asserted that the Russian was in the habit of sitting in a café from five o'clock in the afternoon, arguing with other Russians. But other people declare that he couldn't have been a Russian, because Russians never go home so early as that.

" One day last year, in February it was, I was just dozing off when suddenly I heard the noise of five shots being fired. At first I imagined I was a little boy again and that I was cracking a whip at home in our yard ; and I was very pleased because it made such a nice noise. But then all at once I woke up and realized that somebody was firing a revolver in the street. So I rushed to the window and opened it, and saw a man with a portfolio in his hand lying face downwards on the pavement right in front of No. 7. But at that moment there was a clatter of feet and a policeman appeared round the corner, ran up to the man and tried to lift him up ; then he let him go again, said : ' Damn it ! ' and blew a whistle. Just then another policeman came round the other corner and ran up to the first one.

" As you can imagine, I quickly put on my slippers and overcoat, and rushed down. I was joined by the vegetarian, the banjo-player, one of the goldfish experts, two house-porters and one stamp-collector ; the rest only looked on from their windows, with their teeth chattering, and said to themselves : ' You never know, I might land myself into a scrape if I went down.' Meanwhile the two policemen had turned the man over on to his back.

" ' Why, it's the Russian, Kopytenko or Kovalenko, who lives here at Mrs. Janská's,' I said, with my teeth chattering. ' Is he dead ? '

" ' I don't know,' said one of the policemen, who seemed at his wits' end. ' We shall have to call a doctor.'

" ' What are you letting him lie there for ? ' the banjo-player expostulated with chattering teeth.

" By this time about a dozen of us had collected there and we were shivering with cold and alarm, while the policemen knelt down by the man who had been shot, and for some reason or other loosened his collar. At this moment a taxi stopped at the corner of the street and the driver came up to see what was the matter ; most likely he hoped it was a drunken man whom he could take home.

" ' What you got there, gents ? ' he asked affably.

" ' A man's been sh-sh-shot,' stuttered the vegetarian. ' Put him into your t-t-taxi and take him to the hospital. He may still be alive.'

" ' Blimey,' said the taxi-driver, ' I ain't fond of fares like this. But anyway, if you'll wait a bit, I'll drive up ! '— Then he walked slowly towards his cab and drove up to where we were. ' Put him in there,' he said.

" The two policemen lifted up the Russian and with quite an effort managed to get him into the taxi ; he was rather on the small side, but moving corpses about is an awkward job.

" ' Look here, mate, you go with him, and I'll take down the names of the witnesses,' said the first policeman to the other one. ' Driver, take him to the hospital and be quick about it.'

" ' Be quick about it,' growled the driver, ' that's all very fine with the rotten brakes I've got.' And off he drove.

" The first policeman took a notebook out of his breast-pocket and said : ' You'll have to tell me your names, gentlemen ; it's only on account of the evidence.' And then he wrote our names, one after the other in his notebook, and a dickens of a time he took over it, too ; his fingers may have been numbed, but before he'd finished we were nearly frozen to death. When I got back to my room, it was twenty-five past eleven ; so the whole business had lasted for ten minutes.

" I expect that Mr. Taussig here will think that there's nothing out of the way about this affair, but you know, Mr. Taussig, in a respectable street like ours an affair of that sort is quite a big event. The neighbouring streets sort of enjoy a little reflected glory and tell everyone that it happened only just round the corner ; the streets that are a bit farther off pretend it's all the same to them, but I don't mind telling you that as a matter of fact they're disgusted and annoyed because it didn't happen in their precincts. A couple of turnings farther on they just pooh-pooh the whole thing and say : ' Someone's supposed to have been done in there, but there may be nothing in it.' That's only their low jealousy.

" You can imagine how all of us in that street made a rush for the evening papers next day. For one thing, we wanted to read some new details about our murder, and then we were delighted to think that there would be something in the papers about our street and what had happened to us. It's a well-known fact that what people like to read about most in the papers is something they've seen for themselves, something of which they were what is called eye-witnesses. Suppose for example a horse has fallen down in the street and in consequence there's been a stoppage of the traffic for ten minutes ; if there's nothing in the paper about it, the people who saw it happen grumble at the paper and chuck it into a corner, because they say it has let them down badly.

They almost feel insulted that the paper didn't think it worth while mentioning the accident that they're, so to speak, part-owners of. If you ask me, the only reason why the papers publish items of local news is because if they didn't, the eye-witnesses would be so annoyed that they'd stop taking the paper in.

"I tell you, we were absolutely flabbergasted to find that not a single evening paper so much as mentioned this murder of ours. They're full of all sorts of scandals and confounded rubbish about politics, we grumbled, and there's even a report about a tram that collided with a wheelbarrow, but there's nothing about the murder ; the papers are no damned good anyhow, they're all thoroughly bogus. But then it struck the stamp-collector that the police may have asked the papers not to say anything about the matter for the present, so as not to interfere with their inquiries. That set out minds at rest and at the same time made us more inquisitive than ever ; it made us feel proud to think that we lived in such an important street and that we might be called as witnesses in what was evidently a mysterious business. But the next day the papers still didn't mention it and no-body from the police turned up to make inquiries ; and what struck us as being queerer than anything else was that nobody had called on Mrs. Janská to search or, at least, to seal up the Russian's lodgings. It gave us quite a shock ; the banjo-player said that perhaps the police wanted to hush up the whole business ; 'Heaven alone knows,' he added, 'what there is behind it.' And when on the day after that our murder wasn't mentioned, our street began to protest that something would have to be done about it, that the Russian had been one of us and we were jolly well going to get at the bottom of the business ; that anyhow our street was being victimized in the most barefaced manner ; it was badly paved and badly lighted, and things would look very different if an M.P. or a newspaper-man lived there. And so what with one thing and another, the fat was in the fire, and being the oldest resident and not having any axe to grind, I was deputed to go to the police station and point out how scandalously the murder was being handled.

"So off I went to see Superintendent Bartošek; I know him slightly, he's a glum sort of man—they say it's because he was crossed in love and that's why he joined the police. 'Well, sir,' I said to him, 'I've just come to ask you what's being done about that murder in Krucemburk Street; the people down our way are beginning to wonder why it's being kept so dark.'

" 'What murder?' asked the superintendent. 'No murder's been reported to us here; and that's in our section.'

" 'Why, the other day that Russian Kopytenko or Kovalenko was shot in the street,' I explained to him. 'Two policemen came up and one of them took down our names as witnesses, while the other drove off with the Russian to the hospital.'

" 'What are you talking about?' said the superintendent. 'Nothing's been reported to us. There must be some mistake.'

" 'But there were at least fifty people who saw it,' I said, 'and we can all testify to it '—I began to get annoyed. 'We're respectable citizens, sir; if you tell us to hold our tongues about the murder we'll do the best we can, even if we don't know why. But really, shooting a man in cold blood, that's a little too much; and we'll write to the papers about it.'

" 'Look here,' said Mr. Bartošek, and put on such a stern expression that I was quite scared. 'Just tell me exactly what happened.'

" So I told him exactly what had happened, and presently

he went purple in the face with suppressed rage ; but when
I started telling him how the first policeman had said to the
other one : *Look here, mate, you go with him and I'll take
down the names of the witnesses*—when I told him that, why,
he set up a regular yell, and bellowed : ' I thought as much
—they couldn't have been our men. Damn it all, why
didn't you send for the police and give those policemen in
charge ? Your own common sense ought to have told you
that policemen in uniform never call each other " mate."
The plain-clothes men may do it, but men in uniform, not
in all their born days. You confounded idiot, you ought
to have had those fellows run in.'

" ' But why ? ' I stammered, feeling very small.

" ' Because *they* were the ones who shot the Russian,' the
superintendent roared at me. ' Or at any rate, they had a
hand in it. How long have you been living in Krucemburk
Street ? '

" ' Nine years,' I said.

" ' Then you ought to know that at a quarter past eleven
at night the nearest man on point duty is right down by the
Market Hall and the nearest after that is at the corner of
Slezská Street and Perun Street, and then there's a third
man whose beat is number 1388, and so forth. At that
corner where your policeman came running up, *our* policeman could have come along either at 10.48 or else at 23
minutes after midnight, but not at any other time, because
he's not there at any other time. Why, confound it all,
every burglar knows that, and here are the people who live
on the spot and don't know it. I suppose you think there's
a policeman at every street-corner, don't you ? Why, if
one of our men in uniform had appeared round that confounded corner of yours at the moment you say, there'd be
a fine old rumpus, first of all because at that particular time,
according to regulations, he ought to be on his beat by the

Market Hall, and secondly because he didn't report the murder to us. That'd be a very serious matter, of course.'

" ' Then for goodness' sake,' I said, ' what about the murder ? '

" The superintendent seemed to have calmed down by now, and said : ' That's a different matter ; it looks to me like a very ugly business, Mr. Houdek ; there's a clever brain behind this and a good deal more than meets the eye. They had the whole thing very neatly planned, confound them ! First of all, they knew at what time the Russian used to reach home, then they had the movements of our men at their fingers' ends, and in the third place it gave them two clear days before the police heard anything about the murder—I suppose they wanted to get away in good time or else to put things straight. Now do you understand ? '

" ' Well, not quite,' I said.

" ' Look here,' the superintendent patiently began to explain. ' They dressed up two of their men as policemen, and they waited round the corner to shoot the Russian or till some third person had put a bullet into him. Of course, you were delighted to see how quickly our splendid police were on the spot. By the way,' he interposed, suddenly remembering another detail, ' how did the whistle sound when the first policeman blew it ? '

" ' Rather faint,' I said ; ' but I thought that the policeman had a bit of a cold.'

" ' Aha,' said the superintendent with satisfaction. ' You see, what they wanted was to keep you from reporting the murder to the police ; that gave them time to clear out of the country. And you can bet your life that the taxi-driver was one of the gang, too. I suppose you don't happen to remember the number of the cab ? '

" ' We didn't notice the number,' I said, very crestfallen.

" ' Never mind,' said the superintendent ; ' it's sure to have been a fake ; that gave them a chance of getting rid of the Russian's body. By the way, he wasn't a Russian, but a Macedonian, named Protasov. Well, thanks for coming to see me. But you'd really be doing me a good turn if you said nothing more about this. On account of our investigations, you know. Of course, this is most likely a political job. But there must be a damned clever fellow behind it, because as a rule, Mr. Houdek, these political outrages are arranged very clumsily. Politics, why, it's not even an honest piece of wrongdoing, it's just a vulgar rumpus,' said the superintendent with disgust.

" Later on, a few inquiries were made ; it was never discovered why the murder was committed, but they got the names of the men who did it, only they had cleared out of the country long before. And so our street got completely done out of its murder ; it's just as if somebody had torn out the most glorious page of its history. If some stranger, someone living in Foch Street, say, or someone from the wilds of Vrsovice should happen to come along our way, he probably thinks to himself : ' My word, what a dull street ! ' And nobody believes us when we brag about the mysterious crime that was committed there. The fact is that the other streets begrudge us our murder."

The Musical Conductor's Story

★   ★   ★

"IT's AN awful thing when you want to lend a helping
hand and can't," remarked Kalina, the musical con-
ductor and composer ; " that's what once happened
to me.   It was at Liverpool where I'd been invited to conduct a concert with the orchestra there.   You know, I can't
speak a word of English ; but we musicians can make ourselves understood to each other without a lot of talk,
especially when we've got a baton in our hands.   You just
give a tap with it, shout something, roll your eyes and wave
your arms, and then start all over again.   Even the most
delicate feelings can be expressed like that ; for example,
when I go like that with my arms, everyone can see that it
means a mystical soaring-and-redemption-from-the-burden-
and-sorrow-of life, sort of thing.   Well, when I arrived at
Liverpool, my English friends were waiting for me at the
station and took me off to a hotel, so that I could get a
rest ; but when I'd had a bath, I went out by myself to have
a look at the place, and then I lost my way.

"When I'm in any locality, the first thing I do is to look
for a river ; a river gives you an idea of what I might call
the orchestration of a place.   On one side you have all the
hubbub of the streets, the kettledrums and tympani, the
horns and the brass instruments, while on the other side
there's the river, the strings, a pianissimo of violins and
harps ; there you can hear the whole city at once.   But the
river at Liverpool, I don't know what it's called, but it's all
nasty and yellow ; and this river, let me tell you, fairly
booms and rumbles, roars, howls and clatters, blusters and
hums with ships, tugboats, steamers, warehouses, wharves

and cranes ; you know, I'm immensely fond of ships, whether it's a podgy black tug, or a tramp steamer with a coating of red paint, or one of those white liners. ' Well,' I said to myself, ' hang it all, the sea must be round the corner somewhere, I must go and have a look at it ; and off I went alongside, down the river. I walked and walked for two hours, past nothing but warehouses and sheds and docks ; only here and there a ship could be seen as high as a cathedral, or three stout and slanting funnels ; there was a stench of fish, sweating horses, jute, rum, wheat, coal, iron—you know, where you get a whole lot of iron together, there's quite a regular iron-y smell. I was absolutely delighted ; but by this time, night had fallen and I had reached some sandy flats, a lighthouse was shining opposite and there were tiny lights drifting to and fro—perhaps that was the sea ; then I sat down on a pile of planks and felt so delightfully isolated and lost, I listened to the splashing and the broad murmur of the water and I could have moaned with heartache. Then two people came up, a man and a woman, but they didn't see me ; they sat down with their backs to me and started talking in undertones—if I had understood English, I should have coughed, just to let them know that I could hear ; but as I couldn't speak a word of English, except ' hotel ' and ' shilling,' I lay low.

" First of all they talked very staccato ; then the man began to explain something slowly and softly, as if he was at a loss for words ; and then he wound up his speech with a sudden rush. The woman screamed with horror and spoke some agitated words to him ; but he squeezed her hand till she moaned and began to urge something upon her, talking between his teeth. You know, this wasn't a conversation between lovers ; a musician can tell that ; a lover's attempts at persuasion have quite a different cadence and haven't got that tense sound about them—a conversation between

lovers is a deep 'cello, but this was a high bass, played in a
sort of *presto rubato*, in a single key, as if the man kept
repeating the same phrase.   I began to feel a bit scared at
this : the man was bullying the woman.   She now began to
cry softly and several times uttered a scream as if she was
offering resistance and he was trying to hold her ; her voice
was a little like a clarinet, a reedy voice which didn't sound
quite young ; but the man's voice became harsher and
harsher, as if he was ordering or threatening her.   The
woman's voice began to plead desperately and gasped with
horror, just as a person gasps when you lay an ice-cold
poultice on them ; and I could hear her teeth chattering.
Then the man's voice started murmuring something in very
low tones, a pure bass, almost amorously ; the woman's
crying passed over into short and passive sobs ; that meant
that her opposition had been overcome.   But then the
amorous sound of the bass was uplifted again, and added
phrase to phrase, disjointedly, deliberately, insistently ;
this was accompanied by the woman's voice powerlessly
wailing or sobbing, but now there was no resistance in it,
only a mad fear, not fear of the man, but a bewildered,
uncanny dread of something yet to come.   And then the
man's voice sank down again to a soothing murmur and
gentle threats ; the woman's sobbing changed to dazed and
defenceless sighs ; and in a cold whisper the man asked some
questions to which she evidently replied with a nod, for he
no longer insisted.

" Then the couple got up and separated.

" You know, I don't believe in presentiments, but I
believe in music ; when I was listening there that night, I
knew with absolute certainty that the bass was persuading
the clarinet to be a party to some fearful deed.   I knew that
the clarinet would return home utterly cowed, and would do
what the bass had ordered her to.   I heard that much, and

to hear is more than to understand words. I knew that some crime was afoot, and I knew what it was. I could tell by the horror which oozed from those two voices ; it was in their tinge, in the cadence, the tempo, the pauses, the breaks —you see, music is precise, more precise than speech. The clarinet was too simple to manage anything by itself ; it would only help, it would hand over a key or open a door ; but the harsh, deep bass would do it, while the clarinet was gulping with dread. I dashed off to the town, convinced that something was going to happen, and that I must do something to prevent it ; it is a terrible thing to feel that you are going to arrive too late.

" At last I saw a policeman at a street-corner, and in a sweat and out of breath, I rushed up to him. ' Look here,' I gasped, ' there's a murder being planned in this town.'

" The policeman shrugged his shoulders and said something to me which I did not understand. *Good Lord*, I reminded myself, *he doesn't understand a word I'm saying*.

" ' Murder,' I shouted at him as if he was deaf, and ' don't you understand ? They're going to murder some woman who lives all alone. The servant or the housekeeper will be an accomplice—my God,' I yelled, ' do something, for heaven's sake.'

" The policeman only shook his head and said something that sounded like ' yurvay.'

" ' Now just listen to me,' I tried to explain—I was exasperated and I shook with rage and horror—' this poor woman will open the door to her sweetheart, you can bet your life on that. You simply mustn't let it happen. Search for her.'—At the same time it occurred to me that I did not even know what the woman looked like ; but even if I had known, I couldn't have told him just the same. ' Good God,' I shouted, ' it's an outrage to let it happen.'

" The English policeman looked at me closely, and then apparently tried to appease me. I clutched at my head. ' You fool,' I yelled, beside myself with desperation, ' then I'll find her myself.'

" It was sheer madness, I know, but you see, something's got to be done when a human life's at stake ; I rushed about Liverpool all night to see whether I couldn't discover somebody trying to sneak into a house. It's a queer city, so dreadfully dead at night. . . . Towards morning I sat down on the kerb and sobbed with fatigue ; that's where the policeman found me ; he said ' yurvay ' and took me to my hotel.

" I don't know how I conducted at the rehearsal that morning ; but when at last I flung the baton on the floor and rushed out into the street, the newspaper-boys were shouting the evening papers. I bought one—it contained a big head-line " MURDER " and under that the photograph of a white-haired woman."

The Misadventures of a
Matrimonial Swindler

★　★　★

" I DON'T MIND telling you," said Detective Holub with a modest cough, " that we police authorities don't particularly care for any of these special and out-of-the-way cases ; and we don't particularly care for new-comers, either. An old, well-established criminal, that's quite a different matter ; in the first place we know there and then that he did it, because it's his line of business ; in the second place we know where to find him, and in the third place he doesn't make a lot of fuss and pretend he hasn't done it, because he knows very well that it's all no use. I tell you, gentlemen, it's a fair treat to work with an experienced fellow of that sort. And you can take it from me, too, that in prison these regular criminals are special favourites and they're trusted more than anyone else ; it's these novices and casual wrongdoers who are the worst grumblers and grousers and nothing's good enough for them ; but an old lag knows that quod's a risk of his profession and so it's a waste of time to be a nuisance to himself and others as well. But that's not really what I wanted to talk about.

" About five years ago we were getting reports from up and down the country that an unknown matrimonial swindler was on the rampage. According to the descriptions he was an elderly man, stout and bald, with five gold front-teeth ; he went by the names of Müller, Procházka, Šimek, Šebek, Šinderka, Bilek, Hromádka, Pivoda, Berger, Bejček, Stočes and various others. Well, I'm hanged if this description tallied with any of the matrimonial swindlers we knew, so it was evidently a new-comer. And the boss of our department sent for me and said : ' Holub, you're on railway duty, so wherever you go, just keep a sharp look-out for a fellow with five gold teeth.' All right, I began to look at the teeth of people in trains, and within a fortnight I'd collared three fellows with five gold teeth : they had to prove their identity to me and I'm blowed if one wasn't an inspector of schools and one an M.P., if you please, and I don't need to tell you that I was ticked off by them and also by our people in consequence. That got my back up, and I made up my mind I'd do my damnedest to get hold of the blackguard. It wasn't really my job, but I thought I might as well get my own back on him.

" So I went off on my own to all the orphans and widows who had been swindled out of their money by this crook with the gold teeth under promise of marriage. You wouldn't believe what a lot those victimized orphans and widows had got to say for themselves or how much snivelling they were capable of. But they all agreed at least that he was a well-spoken and respectable fellow and that he had gold teeth and that he showed a fit and proper enthusiasm for domestic bliss ; but there wasn't one of them who'd even taken his finger-prints—it's something shocking how gullible these females are. The eleventh victim—that was at Kamenice—told me with sobs that the gentleman had visited her three times ; he always got there by the train which arrived at 10.35 in the morning, and when he was leaving for the last time, with her money in his pocket, he had looked at the number of her house and said in a tone of surprise : ' Why, just fancy, Miss Marenka, it must be written in the stars that we're going to get married ; the number of your house is 618 and when I come to see you, I always leave by the 6.18 train ; isn't that a good sign ? ' When I heard this, I said to myself : ' It is a good sign and no mistake.' And there and then I took out a railway time-table and looked to see from what station there was a train leaving at 5.18 and giving a connection with the train which reached Kamenice at 10.35. When I'd compared and checked everything, I found that it was most likely to be the train leaving Byst̆rice-Novoves. A railway detective, you see, has to have trains at his fingers' ends.

"As you may suppose, the first day off I had, I went to Byst̆rice-Novoves and inquired whether any stout gentleman with gold stoppings was travelling to and fro from there at all frequently. 'Yes,' said the station-master, 'there's Mr. Lacina, a commercial traveller who lives here in the street down yonder; he got back here only yesterday evening.' So off I went to find this Mr. Lacina; in the passage I ran into a nice, tidy little woman and I said to her: 'Does Mr. Lacina live here?' 'That's my husband,' she said; 'but he's just having a nap after his lunch.' 'Never mind,' I said, and in I went. There was a man lying on the sofa in his shirt sleeves and he said: 'Well, I'm blowed, if it isn't Mr. Holub; give him a chair, ma.'

"At that moment all my ill-feeling vanished; why, it was Plichta, the old lottery-swindler, you know, the one who worked all those frauds with lottery-tickets. This fellow Plichta had been in quod at least ten times. 'Hallo, how are you, old man?' I said. 'So you've given up the lottery stunt.'

"'Ah, that I have,' said Plichta, and sat down on the sofa. 'Mr. Holub, it means a lot of running about, don't it? And I ain't as young as what I was. Fifty-two last birthday I was, and it's about time to settle down a bit; all this trapseing from house to house, that's no job for me now.'

"'That's why you're trying your hand at matrimonial swindles, you humbug,' I said to him.

"Plichta just sighed. 'Mr. Holub,' he said, 'a man's got to do something. You know, the last time I was in quod, there was something went wrong with my teeth ; I think it must be the beans that does it. So I had to have 'em seen to, and you'd be surprised, Mr. Holub, how it sets a man up when he's got gold teeth. It sort of rouses confidence and your digestion improves and you put on flesh. Well, there you are, the likes of us have just got to work with what they've got.'

" ' And what have you done with the money ? ' I asked him. ' I've got particulars of eleven of your frauds in my notebook and it makes a total of two hundred and sixteen thousand crowns clear profit. Where is it ? '

" ' Oh, but, Mr. Holub,' said Plichta, ' all that belongs to my wife. Business is business. I've got nothing except what's on me ; that's six hundred and fifty crowns, a gold watch and my gold teeth. Ma, I'm just off to Prague with Mr. Holub. Look here, Mr. Holub, I've got some instalments to pay off on those teeth ; there's still three hundred crowns owing. I'll leave the money here.'

" ' And you owe your tailor a hundred and fifty crowns,' his wife reminded him.

" ' So I do,' said Plichta. ' Mr. Holub, I'm a great stickler for accuracy. There's nothing like having everything shipshape, is there ? When you've got no debts, you can look every one in the face. That's all part of the job, Mr. Holub. Ma, just give my overcoat a bit of a brush down, so as I shan't be a discredit to you in Prague. Well, Mr. Holub, we may as well be off.'

" So then Plichta got five months. Most of the women, if you please, told the court they'd given him the money of their own free will and that they'd forgive him for what he'd done. But there was one old girl who wouldn't let bygones be bygones, and she was a rich widow he'd only got five thousand from.

" Six months later I heard that there had been two more matrimonial swindles going on. That must be Plichta, I said to myself, but I didn't trouble any further about it. Just at that time I was busy at the railway-station in Pardubice, because a trunk-man was on the job there, you know, one of those fellows who steal luggage from the platform. And as my family was spending their summer holidays in a village barely an hour's journey from Pardubice, I packed some sausages and a few odds and ends of that sort into a handbag for them ; you know, in a village, it's difficult to get hold of victuals like that. And while I was on my way, I walked right through the train, as I always do ; and there, in one of the compartments, sat Plichta with an elderly lady and he was saying something about what a corrupt place the world is.

" ' Hallo, old man,' I said, ' are you promising marriage to some one again ? '

" Plichta turned red and hastily asked the lady to excuse him, because he had to see a gentleman on business ; and when he'd joined me in the corridor, he said reproachfully : ' Mr. Holub, you oughtn't to have done that in front of strangers ; it would have been enough if you'd tipped me the wink—I'd have come. What do you want me for ? '

" ' We've got a couple more cases on hand, Plichta,' I said to him. ' But I've got another job to-day, so I'll hand you over to the gendarmes at Pardubice.'

" ' Oh, Mr. Holub, don't treat me like that ; I'm quite used to you now and you know me too—I'd rather come with you. Do me the favour, Mr. Holub, just for old times' sake.'

" ' It can't be managed,' I said. ' I'm going first of all to visit my family, and it'll take me about an hour to get there. What could I do with you in the meantime ? '

" ' I'll come with you, Mr. Holub,' suggested Plichta. ' Anyway, then the journey won't seem so long to you.'

" So Plichta came with me, and I introduced him to my wife and sister-in-law as an old friend of mine. I tell you, my sister-in-law is quite a good-looking girl and she's only twenty-five, but Plichta's talk was so nice and gentlemanly and he gave the children sweets—well, to cut a long story short, when we'd drunk our coffee Mr. Plichta suggested that he'd go for a stroll with the young lady and the children, and just tipped me the wink as much as to say, we fellows understand each other, and I'd probably want to have a talk with my missus. That's the sort of high-minded chap he was. And when they got back an hour later, the children were holding Mr. Plichta's hand, my sister-in-law was all blushes, and when we left she squeezed his hand quite a long time.

" ' Look here, Plichta,' I said to him afterwards, ' what do you mean by putting ideas into Manicka's head ? '

" ' That's just habit,' said Plichta almost sadly. ' Mr. Holub, I can't help it, it's the teeth that does it. It's always getting me into trouble, you see. I never flirt with ladies, it wouldn't do for a man of my age, but there you are, that's just what makes them all the keener. Sometimes I can't help wondering whether they really like me for myself alone, or if it's only greed, because I look well off.'

" When we got back to the railway station at Pardubice, I said to him, ' Look here, Plichta, I'm afraid I shall have to hand you over to the gendarmes now, because I've got to investigate a case of theft.'

" ' Mr. Holub, you might as well let me take a seat in the refreshment-room here,' pleaded Plichta. ' I'll have some tea and read the papers—here's my money, fourteen thousand crowns and a bit ; and without money I can't run away—why, I couldn't even pay my bill.'

" So I let him take a seat in the refreshment-room and went off on my job. An hour later I had a look through the window ; he was sitting where I left him, he had a pair of gold pince-nez on his nose and he was reading a newspaper. About half an hour after that I was ready and went to fetch him. By that time he was sitting at the next table with an outsize blonde and was telling the waiter off in a very dignified manner for putting curdled milk into her coffee. When he saw me, he took his leave of the lady and came across to me. ' Mr. Holub,' he said, ' couldn't you give me another week before you run me in ? There's a job here I could just about do.'

" ' Very rich ? ' I asked him.

" Plichta made a sign with his hand. ' Mr. Holub,' he whispered, ' she's got a factory ; and what she very much needs is an experienced man to advise her now and then. She's just got to pay for some new machinery.'

" ' Aha, my boy, come along then, let me introduce you. How do you do, Gladys, still chasing after elderly gentlemen ? '

" The blonde turned red to the roots of her hair and said : ' My gracious, Mr. Holub, I didn't know this gentleman was a friend of yours.'

" ' Now make yourself scarce,' I said to her. ' There's a certain Mr. Dundr who'd like to have a word with you ; he calls your little game fraud, you know.'

" Plichta was flabbergasted. ' Mr. Holub,' he said, ' I'd never have believed that this lady was a crook too.'

" ' Well, she is,' I said to him, ' and no better than she ought to be, in the bargain ; let me tell you that she wheedles money out of elderly gentlemen under promise of marriage.'

" Plichta went as white as a sheet. ' Well, I'm hanged ! ' he said, and spat with disgust. ' Catch me trusting women after that. Mr. Holub, that's really the limit.'

" ' Now you just wait here,' I said, ' and I'll get you a ticket to Prague. Second or third class ? '

" ' Mr. Holub,' protested Plichta, ' that'd be a waste of money. Being in custody, I'm entitled to a free ticket, aren't I ? Then take me along at Government expense. A man in my position has got to be careful of every penny.'

" All the way to Prague, Plichta was cursing and swearing about that woman ; it was the deepest moral indignation I've ever come across. When we got out at Prague, Plichta said : ' Mr. Holub, I know that this time it'll be seven months ; and prison food don't agree with me. Look here, I'd like to have one more square feed while I can. That fourteen thousand you took away from me was all I cleared over my last job—I ought to have at least one dinner out of it ; and I'd like to stand you a coffee for the one I had from you.'

" So we went along together to a pretty good restaurant ; Plichta ordered something from the grill and drank five beers and I paid for it out of his purse, while he went over the bill three times to make sure the waiter wasn't overcharging us.

" ' Right you are, and now off we go to where the cops hang out,' I said.

" ' Wait a bit, Mr. Holub,' said Plichta. ' I had a lot of overhead expenses in connection with that last job. There were four journeys there and back at 48 crowns each —that makes 384 crowns.' Then he put on his pince-nez and did some calculations on a piece of paper. ' Then out-of-pocket expenses, say 30 crowns a day—I've got to keep up appearances, Mr. Holub, that's all part of my stock-in-trade. So that makes 120 crowns. Then I gave the young lady a bunch of flowers that cost me 35 crowns—just as an act of politeness, you know. The engagement ring cost 240—it was only gilt, Mr. Holub; if I wasn't an honest man, I'd tell you it was gold, and reckon the cost at 600, wouldn't I ? Then I bought her a cake for 30 crowns; next we have the postage on five letters, that's one crown each, and the advertisement by which I got to know her cost 80 crowns. That makes a grand total of 832 crowns, Mr. Holub. You really must deduct that for me, and I'll leave the money with you for the time being. I like to have everything just so. Mr. Holub, we must at least cover our overhead expenses. That's the lot, and now we can be off.'

" And when we were in the passage at police headquarters, Plichta suddenly remembered one more item : ' Mr. Holub, I gave the young lady a bottle of scent ; that makes another twenty crowns to my credit.'

" Then he carefully blew his nose, and with his mind at rest let them take him off."

The Epic Exploit of Juraj Čup

★　　★　　★

"YES, IT does sometimes happen," said Captain Havelka of the gendarmes, "that criminals turn out to be remarkably conscientious and straightforward. I could give you lots of examples to prove it, but the queerest one was the experience I had with a man named Juraj Čup. It happened when I was stationed with the gendarmes at Jasina in Ruthenia.

"One night in January we had a bit of a spree at the local inn; there was a district governor, a railway manager and some bigwigs looking after the interests of the Republic in those remote parts; and, of course, there were gypsies. You know about these gypsies; I'm hanged if I can make out where they're descended from, but sometimes I think they must belong to the tribe of Ham. When they come up and play the fiddle in front of you, nearer and nearer, and softer and softer, the uncanny devils, when their hocus-pocus finds its way into your ear, when—when you feel as if they're dragging your soul away from your body; I tell you, that music of theirs, it's like some awful and uncanny vice. And when they came right up close to me, I cried, I yelled at the top of my voice, I stuck my bayonet through the table, I smashed glasses, I sang and I banged my head against the wall, I felt as if I must kill someone or make love to someone—that's the sort of tricks a man gets up to when the gypsies have put a spell on him. And when I was in the thick of it all, the landlord came up and said that there was some Ruthenian or other waiting for me outside in front of the inn.

" ' Let him wait or come back to-morrow,' I yelled ; ' here am I lamenting for my youth and burying my dreams ; there's a lady, a great and beautiful lady I'm in love with— play, you rascal of a gypsy, play on, and drive the sorrow out of my soul '—that's the kind of thing I said ; you know, it all goes with the music, all that sense of despair and the drinking on a terrific scale. An hour later the landlord came back and said that the Ruthenian was still waiting for me outside, where it was freezing hard. But I hadn't finished lamenting my youth and I hadn't yet managed to drown my sorrows in Tokay ; so I just waved my hand like a Jenghis Khan, as much as to say, I don't care what becomes of me, play on, gypsies ; and what happened after that, I don't know, but when I went outside towards morning, it was freezing so hard that the snow crunched and tinkled like glass, and there in front of the tavern, stood the Ruthenian in white bast-shoes, white breeches and a white sheepskin. When he saw me, he curtsied to the waist, and said something in a hoarse voice.

" ' What do you want ? ' I said to him.   ' If you waste my time, you'll feel the weight of my hand across your mouth.'

" ' Your honour,' said the Ruthenian, ' I've been sent here by the mayor of Volová Lehota. Marina Matejova has been killed.'

" That sobered me up a bit.   Volová Lehota was a village, or rather a lonely cluster of about thirty huts, fifteen miles or so farther up among the mountains ; a pleasant trip to look forward to with the thermometer well below zero. ' Good God,' I shouted, ' and who killed her ? '

" ' I did, your honour,' said the Ruthenian meekly.   ' My name is Juraj Čup, the son of Dmitri Čup.'

" ' And you've come to give yourself up,' I blurted out.

" ' The mayor ordered me to,' said Juraj Čup sub-missively. ' Juraj, he said, go and tell the gendarme that you killed Marina Matejova.'

" ' And why did you kill her ? ' I shouted.

" ' God ordered it,' said Juraj, as though it were a matter of course. ' The Lord commanded : Kill Marina Matejova, your sister, who is possessed by an evil spirit.'

" ' Damn and blast you ! ' I said, ' but how did you get here from Volová Lehota ? '

" ' With God's help,' said Juraj Čup piously. ' The Lord protected me so that I might not perish in the snow. Praised be His name.'

" Now if you knew what a blizzard is like in the Carpathians, if you knew what it means to have a good six feet of snow on the ground ; if you could have seen that puny and feeble little fellow Juraj Čup who'd been waiting for six hours in front of the inn in all that fearful cold to give himself up for having murdered Marina Matejova, God's unworthy handmaiden, I wonder what you'd have done ; what I did was to cross myself, Juraj Čup crossed himself, and then I arrested him ; then I washed my face in the snow, fastened on my snow-shoes and with a gendarme, named Kroupa, off we went up the mountains to Volová Lehota. And if the commander-in-chief of the gendarmes himself had stopped me and said : ' Havelka, you're crazy, you'll never get there ; why, in this snow, your life isn't safe '—I'd have saluted and said : ' Beg to report, sir, it's the Lord's orders.' And off I'd have gone. And so would Kroupa, because he was from Žižkov ; and I've never met a man from Žižkov who didn't want to show off and be in the thick of it when there was anything plucky or foolhardy afoot. So off we went.

" I won't describe this trip of ours to you ; I'll merely

tell you that at the end of it Kroupa was sobbing like a child with fright and fatigue, and that twice we'd told ourselves that it was all up with us and that we couldn't budge another inch ; also, it took us eleven hours, from one night to another, to go those fifteen miles ; I just mention this to give you an idea of what it was like.   A gendarme's a tough customer, gentlemen, and when even he falls down in the snow and starts sobbing that he can't move any farther—well, it means that things are too bad to describe.   But I just walked on and on, as if I was asleep, and all I did was to keep reminding myself that Juraj Čup had managed it, Juraj Čup, a weedy little man, and on top of that he had waited for six hours in the bitter cold, because the mayor had told him to ; Juraj Čup in his wet bast-shoes, Juraj Čup in the blizzard, Juraj Čup trusting in God's help.   You know, if you saw a stone falling upwards instead of downwards, you'd call it a miracle ; but nobody gives the name of miracle to that journey which Juraj Čup made so as to give himself up ; and yet it was a more wonderful thing and a more awe-inspiring sign of strength than a stone falling upwards. And let me tell you this much, that if you want to see miracles, you've got to look at men and not at stones.

" Well, when we got to Volová Lehota, we were staggering along like shadows, more dead than alive.   We knocked at the mayor's door ; everyone was asleep.   Presently the mayor came creeping out with a rifle ; he was a huge man with a beard, and when he saw us, he kneeled down and un-fastened our snow-shoes, but he never spoke a word.   When I recall what happened, I seem to see a strange set of images, all reduced to a solemn simplicity : the mayor silently leading us into one of the huts ; two candles burning in the room, a woman in black kneeling before an ikon, on a bed the corpse of Marina Matejova in a white shroud, with her throat cut from ear to ear ; it was a fearful wound and yet it was a strangely clean one, just as when a butcher slits a sucking-pig in two ; and the face was an eerie white, as only those can be who have been drained of their last drop of blood.

" Then, still silent, the mayor led us back to his own dwelling, but in his hut there were eleven peasants waiting, all of them dressed in fur coats. I wonder whether you know what the smell of these sheepskin garments is like ; there's something stifling and Old Testamenty about it. The mayor made us sit down at the table, cleared his throat, bowed and said : ' In the name of God we grieve to tell you of the death of Marina Matejova, the servant of God. May the Lord be merciful to her ! '

" ' Amen,' said the eleven rustics, and crossed themselves.

" And the mayor began. Two days ago in the night-time he had heard someone outside scratching, softly scratching at the door. He thought it was a fox ; so he took his gun and went to open the door. On the threshold lay a woman. It was Marina Matejova with her throat cut. As her windpipe was severed, she was dumb.

" The mayor carried Marina into his hut and laid her on the bed, then he ordered the shepherd to blow his bugle and summon all the peasants of Volová Lehota to him. When they had assembled, he turned to Marina and said : ' Marina Matejova, before you die, bear witness who killed you. Marina Matejova, did I kill you ? '

" Marina could not shake her head ; but she closed her eyes.

" Marina, was it this man here, your neighbour Vlaho, the son of Vasil ? '

" Marina closed her plaintive eyes.

" ' Marina Matejova, was it the peasant Kohut here, known as Vaňka ? Was it Martin Dudáš here, your neighbour ?—Marina, was it this one, Baran, known as Šandor ?

—Marina, was it the one standing here, Andrej Vorobec?
—Marina Matejova, was it Klimbo Bezuchy, who is standing
before you? Marina, was it this man, Štěpan Bobot?—
Marina, was the one who killed you Tatka, the gamekeeper,
the son of Mihal Tatka? Marina——'

" At that moment the door opened and in came Juraj
Čup, the brother of Marina Matejova. Marina trembled
and her eyes started out of her head.

" ' Marina,' continued the mayor, ' who killed you? Was
it this one here, Fodor, whose name is Terentik? '

" But Marina did not answer. ' Say your prayers,' said
Juraj Čup, and all the peasants fell on their knees. At
last the mayor stood up and said : ' Let the women in.'

" ' Not yet,' said old Dudáš. ' Marina Matejova, the
servant of God, now no more, in the name of God give a sign :
Did Duro the shepherd kill you? '

" There was silence.

" ' Marina Matejova, whose soul is with the Lord, did
Tóth Ivan, the son of Ivan, kill you? '

" Nobody breathed.

" ' Marina Matejova, in the name of God, then it was your
brother, Juraj Čup, who killed you? '

" ' I killed her,' said Juraj Čup. ' The Lord commanded
me ; kill Marina, who is possessed by an evil spirit.'

" ' Close her eyelids,' ordered the mayor. ' Juraj, you
will now go to Jasina and give yourself up to the gendarmes.
You will say to them : *I have killed Marina Matejova.*
Until then you will neither sit down nor eat. Go, Juraj.'—
Then he opened the door and let the women into the hut to
lament over the dead.

" Well, I don't know whether it was those sheepskins or
fatigue or because there was something queerly beautiful or
dignified in what I had seen and heard, but I had to go outside in the bitter cold, because my head was in a whirl ; upon

M

my soul, something rose up inside me, as if I ought to get up and say : ' God's people, God's people ! We will judge Juraj Čup according to human laws, but within you is the law of God.' And I could have bowed down low before them, but that would never do for a gendarme, and so I just went out and swore away all on my own until I was in a gendarme's frame of mind again.

" You know, it's a rough job being a gendarme. In the morning I ransacked Juraj Čup's hut and fished out the dollar bank-notes that poor Marina had been getting from her husband in America. Of course, I had to report it, and those lawyer fellows worked it up into a case of murder and larceny. Juraj Čup was hanged ; but nobody's going to persuade me that he managed that journey by human strength. I know exactly what human strength amounts to. And I fancy I've got an inkling of what God's judgment is."

Giddiness

*   *   *

"CONSCIENCE," SAID Mr. Lacina, " is a word that's no longer used. Now they call it repressions, but it's six of one and half a dozen of the other. I don't know whether any of you remember the case of Gierke, the factory-owner. He was very wealthy, a splendid fellow too, a fine figure of a man. They said he was a widower, but beyond that nothing was known about him ; he had such a reserved disposition. When he was well over forty, he fell in love with a dainty little slip of a girl ; she was only seventeen and so pretty that it made you hold your breath when you looked at her ; the real kind of prettiness makes your heart feel a twinge of sorrow or tenderness or whatever it is. So this was the girl that Gierke married, because he was the great and wealthy Gierke.

" They went to Italy for their honeymoon and this is what happened there : At Venice they climbed up on to the famous campanile, and when Gierke looked down—they say it's a very fine view—he went all pale, turned towards his young wife, and collapsed as if he'd been felled to the ground. After that he became more reserved than ever ; he tried fearfully hard to make it seem as if there was nothing the matter with him, but his eyes had a restless and desperate look. As you can imagine, his wife became terribly scared and took him back home ; they had a fine house looking out on the park, and it was there that Gierke's queerness got worse and worse. He used to go from window to window, to make sure that they were properly fastened, and hardly had he sat down, than he'd jump up

177

again to go and close some window or other. Even in the night he'd get up and wander like a ghost all over the house —in reply to every question he just muttered that he was confoundedly giddy and that he wanted to shut the windows so as he shouldn't fall out of them. So then his wife had gratings put across all the windows, to rid him of this perpetual nervousness. For a few days it answered its purpose, Gierke calmed down a bit, but then he started rushing about again from window to window and shook the gratings to make sure that they would hold. Then they had steel shutters fixed and lived behind them as if they were boarded up. This made Gierke a little quieter, but then it turned out that he became giddy when he had to walk on the staircase ; so when he went upstairs or down, they had to guide him and hold him by the arm as if he were a cripple ; and even then he trembled like a leaf, and was drenched with sweat ; in fact, sometimes he had to sit down in the middle of the stairs, and he'd burst into a fit of sobs, he was in such a terrible state of fear.

" Of course, they began to consult all sorts of doctors about it, and as generally happens in cases like that, one bone-setter said that the attacks of giddiness were due to overwork, another one explained that it was a disease known as labyrinthitis, a third put it down to constipation, while a fourth expressed the view that it was caused by an insufficiency of blood in the brain ; you know, I've always noticed that as soon as anyone becomes a prominent specialist, by some inner process there's first of all a standpoint makes its appearance inside him. A specialist like that will say : From my standpoint, of course, things are so and so. Whereupon the other specialist will object : But from my standpoint the case is diametrically opposite. My view is that standpoints ought to be left in the entrance hall, like hats and sticks; as soon as you allow a man with a standpoint to get anywhere, then as sure as eggs are eggs, he'll do some mischief, or at the very least, he'll disagree with everybody else. But to come back to Gierke, every month he was treated and tortured by a fresh prominent specialist, each time according to an entirely different method. Gierke was a strapping fellow and could stand it; but the time came when he couldn't get up out of his arm-chair, because he used to have a fit of giddiness as soon as he looked at the ground, and so he just stared into vacancy, without speaking or moving, except that sometimes he'd just shake all over ; that was when he wept.

"At this juncture, a new doctor, a neurologist began to perform miracles—Spitz his name was ; this Dr. Spitz based his method on the treatment of these repressions. You see, his argument was that everybody in their subconsciousness has all sorts of awful ideas or memories or cravings that he represses because he's afraid of them : and these repressed ideas play old Harry inside him, and get things in a mess and cause these nervous disturbances ; and when a doctor who knows his job gropes about till he drags this repression out into the light of day, the patient gets relieved and is all right again. But a psychoanalytical medico has to gain the absolute confidence of the patient he's treating, and gets him to hold forth about all kinds of things : what he dreams at night, what he remembers of his life as a baby, and so on. And he winds up by saying to him : Why, my dear good man, years and years ago you had such and such an experience—generally it's something very scandalous—and that's been sticking in your subconscious, it's what we call a psychic trauma ; but now you've got rid of it, ena dena dina do, hocus-pocus and you're well again. That's the sort of magic it is.

"Now this Dr. Spitz really did things by magic. You wouldn't believe what a lot of repressions rich people have ;

poor people as a rule aren't troubled that way. And so, Dr. Spitz had a huge practice. Well, after all the medical big-wigs in turn had tried what they could do with Gierke, Dr. Spitz was called in ; and Dr. Spitz declared that those attacks of giddiness were of nervous origin and that he, Hugo Spitz, guaranteed to rid the patient of them. Very well, then. The only thing was that Gierke, confound him, wasn't exactly talkative ; whatever Dr. Spitz asked him about, he could scarcely get a word out of him in reply, and then he'd hold his tongue completely. The end of it was that he showed Dr. Spitz the door. Dr. Spitz was in despair ; hang it all, an important patient like that means a lot in the way of prestige. Besides, it was a particularly attractive and ticklish case of nervous breakdown. More-over, Irma—that was Mrs. Gierke—was a very pretty and also a very unhappy woman. And so Dr. Spitz got his teeth well into it. ' I'm going to discover that repression of Gierke's,' he growled, ' or I'll drop medicine and get a job in a draper's shop.'

" So then he started off on a new psycho-analytical method. First of all he traced all Gierke's aunts, cousins, brothers-in-law and other elderly relatives, both close and distant, who were still alive ; then he proceeded to gain their confidence—one of the first things a medical man has to learn is how to listen patiently. These relatives were de-lighted to find how charming and deferential Dr. Spitz was to them ; but the end of it was that Dr. Spitz began to pull a very long face and applied to a certain confidential agency which dispatched two reliable persons to some destination or other. When they came back, Dr. Spitz paid them for their trouble and went straight to Mr. Gierke. Gierke was sitting in an arm-chair in semi-darkness ; he was now scarcely able to move a limb.

" 'Mr. Gierke,' said Dr. Spitz to him, ' I'm not going to

worry you ; you needn't answer me a single word.   I won't
ask you about anything.   All I want to do is to remove the
cause of your attacks of giddiness.   You have thrust it down
into your subconscious ; but the repression is so strong that
it produces serious disturbances——'

" ' I didn't send for you, doctor,' Gierke hoarsely interrupted him, and stretched his hand out towards the bell.

" ' I know,' said Dr. Spitz, ' but just wait a moment.
When you first had that fit of giddiness on the campanile at
Venice, try and remember what your feelings were at the
time.'

" Gierke sat there rigidly with his finger on the bell.

" ' What you felt was,' continued Dr. Spitz—' what you
felt was a dreadful, mad craving to throw your beautiful
young wife down from the belfry.   But because you were
tremendously in love with her, a conflict arose within you
and came to a head in the form of a mental shock ; you
collapsed with giddiness.'

" Not a sound was heard ; the hand that was stretched
out towards the bell suddenly sank down.

" ' Ever since then,' Dr. Spitz went on, ' this giddiness,
this dread of the abyss, has become chronic with you, ever
since then you keep the windows closed and have found it
impossible to look down from a height, because you were
haunted by the dreadful idea that you might push Mrs.
Gierke down—— '

" Gierke in his arm-chair gave a moan which was not
human.

" ' Yes,' continued Dr. Spitz, ' but the question now is,
where did this obsession come from ?   Mr. Gierke, you were
first married eighteen years ago.   Mr. Gierke, your first
wife perished on a tour in the Alps.   She fell over a precipice
while climbing the Hohe Wand and you inherited her
property.'

" Gierke's rapid and wheezy breathing was the only sound that could be heard.

" ' Gierke,' exclaimed Dr. Spitz, ' you murdered your first wife. You pushed her over the precipice ; and that's why, I tell you, that's why you've got the idea that you'll have to kill the second one as well, the one you're in love with ; that's why you're afraid of heights ; that's why you're troubled with giddiness——'

" ' Doctor,' wailed the man in the arm-chair, ' doctor, what am I to do ? What am I to do to stop it ? '

" Dr. Spitz looked terribly upset. ' Mr. Gierke,' he said, ' if I were a religious man, I'd advise you to give yourself up, so that God might have mercy on your soul. But as a rule we doctors don't believe in God. You'll have to settle with yourself as to what you're to do, but from a medical point of view, it's evident that you're saved. Stand up, Mr. Gierke.'

" Gierke stood up, as white as a sheet.

" ' Well,' said Dr. Spitz, ' is your head in a whirl ? '

" Gierke shook his head.

" ' There you are, you see,' Dr. Spitz sighed with relief. ' Now the other symptoms will disappear too. That giddiness was only the result of a repression ; now that we've got rid of it, you'll be all right. Can you look out of the window ? Excellent ! It makes you feel as if you'd thrown everything off. Not a trace of giddiness, eh ? Mr. Gierke, you're the finest case I've ever had.' Dr. Spitz rubbed his hands together with delight. ' Entirely cured. May I call Mrs. Gierke ? No ? Ah, I see, you want to give her a surprise all by yourself. My word, won't she be pleased when she sees you walking. There you are, Mr. Gierke, just see what miracles science can perform ? '—In his sheer joy at his success he would have gone on chattering for a couple of hours, but he saw that Gierke needed rest ; so he prescribed some bromide for him and took his leave.

" ' I'll see you to the door, doctor,' said Gierke politely, and went with the doctor to the staircase.

" ' That's strange, not a sign of any giddiness, not a sign——'

" ' That's first rate,' exclaimed Dr. Spitz effusively ; ' then you feel quite well, eh ? '

" ' Absolutely well,' said Gierke softly, and looked down at the doctor. And when the front door had closed noisly behind Dr. Spitz, there was just a heavy thud.

" After a while they discovered Gierke's body below the staircase. He was dead ; several of his limbs had been broken through his having been hurled against the balustrade of the staircase while falling.

" When Dr. Spitz was told about it, he whistled to himself and made a very peculiar face. Then he took the book in which he entered the names of his patients, and opposite Gierke's name he just added the date and the one word ' *suicidum.*' And you can guess what that means, Mr. Taussig."

Confessional

★　　★　　★

"WITH REGARD to repressions," remarked Father Voves of St. Matthew's, "you know, curing these repressions is one of the oldest of human experiences; the only thing is that our holy church calls this method of healing 'sacramentum sanctæ confessionis.' When something is oppressing your soul, when there is something you are ashamed of, go, poor sinful wretch, to holy confession and make a clean breast of the filth which you are carrying about with you. The only thing is that we don't call this curing nervous disturbances, we call it remorse, repentance and forgiveness of sins.

"Now, many years ago, on a sweltering hot summer's day, I had withdrawn into my church—you know, it always seems to me that the Evangelicals could have come into existence only in northern countries where, even in summer, nobody feels the heat. In any one of our Catholic churches there is something for you the livelong day—mass, matins, vespers, or, if nothing else, the pictures and statues; at any time you can drop in, enjoy the cool air and indulge in meditation—but this can only be appreciated when it's as hot as an oven outside. That's why you get the dissenters in cold and inhospitable countries and us Catholics in the warmer regions; that's probably due to the cool and shady atmosphere in the holy places of the Lord. Well, as I was saying, it was a broiling day; when I entered the church, something beautiful and soothing was wafted towards me. And then the verger came up and told me that a man had been waiting there for more than an hour to be confessed.

"Well, of course, that often happens; so I fetched my surplice from the sacristy and sat down in the box. The verger brought the penitent along—he was an elderly man, quite decently dressed. He looked like a commercial traveller or an estate agent, and his face was pale and rather bloated. He kneeled down by the confessional-box and said nothing.

"'Now then,' I said to encourage him, 'say this after me: I, a wretched sinner, confess and acknowledge unto God Almighty——'

"'No,' the man rapped out, 'I've got a different way of saying it. Let me do it my way. I must say it differently.' Suddenly his chin began to tremble and sweat broke out on his forehead; and I too, for no reason whatever, began to feel a strange and horrible sense of loathing — only once before had I ever felt the same sort of shock and that was when I was present at the exhumation of a corpse which was . . . which was already in a state of decay. I'm not going to tell you, gentlemen, what it was like.

"'For Heaven's sake, what's the matter with you?' I exclaimed, quite alarmed.

"'Just a moment, just a moment,' stammered the man; he gave a deep sigh, blew his nose noisily and said: 'It's all right now. Well, your Reverence, I'll begin. Twelve years ago . . .'

"I won't tell you what he said. In the first place, of course, it's the secret of the confessional; and then, too, it was so ghastly, so repulsive and bestial an act that—well, it couldn't be repeated; and that man blurted it all out in such appalling detail—he left nothing to the imagination, nothing whatever. I thought I'd have to run away from the confessional-box, and stop up my ears or something; I stuffed my surplice into my mouth to prevent myself from uttering a shout of horror.

" ' Well, now that's off my chest,' said the man in a satisfied tone, and he blew his nose with relief. ' Thanks, your Reverence.'

" ' Wait a bit,' I exclaimed, ' and what about penance ? '

" ' What do you take me for ? ' said the man, and peeped at me through the small window almost familiarly. ' Padre, I don't believe in anything ; I just came to ease my feelings. You know, when I've not talked about . . . about that business for some time, then I see . . . the whole thing before me . . . and I can't sleep, I can't close an eye. And when I get that way, I have to make a clean breast of it, I have to tell someone about it ; and that's what you're here for, that's your job and you've got to keep it to yourself —it's a secret of the confessional. But as for absolution, I don't care a rap about that ; that's no go, when you haven't got any faith. Well, many thanks, your Reverence. My best respects.' And before I realized what was happening, he was strutting jauntily out of the church.

" About a year later, he turned up again. He button-holed me in front of the church ; he was pale and exceedingly humble. ' Your Reverence,' he stammered, ' may I confess to you ? '

" ' Look here,' I said to him, ' it can't be done without penance, and there's an end of it. If you won't atone, we can't do any business together.'

" ' Good heavens,' sighed the man, looking very crest-fallen, ' that's what every padre tells me now. There's not one of them who'll confess me, and I need it so badly. I say, your Reverence, what does it matter to you, if I—if I just once more——'

" With that his lips began to tremble as before. ' It can't be done,' I exclaimed angrily, 'unless you tell me the whole thing in the presence of some layman.'

" And then in the midst of spasms and gasps it all came out. I tell you, I'd never heard anything like it."

" Hm, hm," coughed Baum the barrister.

" Don't be scared," said Dr. Vitásek, " I'm not going to tell you what it was, that's a medical secret. Afterwards he lay there like a wet rag, absolutely exhausted. You know, I couldn't give him absolution or any wise advice, your Reverence, but I gave him a couple of doses of morphia and when he woke up, another couple, and then again, until he didn't wake up any more. I gave him a helping hand with a vengeance, let me tell you."

" Amen," said Father Voves, and meditated a little. " That was fine of you," he added softly ; " you did at least put him out of his misery."

Mr. Havlena's Verdict

★ ★ ★

" TALKING ABOUT newspapers," said Mr. Beran, " what I think is this : Most people turn first of all to the police reports. It's hard to say whether they're so keen on reading them because of a suppressed desire to commit crime, or for their moral satisfaction and to increase their knowledge of law. What is certain is that they just gloat over them. That's why the papers have to publish police reports every day. But now suppose, for example, the court vacations are on ; the courts aren't sitting, but there's got to be a column of reports about them just the same. Or often enough there are no sensational cases on at any of the courts and the police-news reporter has got to have a sensational case, by hook or by crook. When things are like that, the reporters simply have to hatch out a sensational case for themselves. There's a regular market for these sham cases and they're bought, lent or exchanged at the rate of twenty cigarettes or so per item. I know all about it, because I used to share diggings with a police-news reporter ; he was fond of booze and he was a slacker, but apart from that he was a fellow who had all his wits about him and who had a miserable screw.

" Now one day a queer sort of chap, down-at-heels, dirty and bloated, turned up in the café where the police-news reporters used to meet ; his name was Havlena, he'd studied law but never finished it and he had altogether gone to the dogs ; nobody knew exactly how he made a living—in fact, he didn't quite know himself. Well, this fellow Havlena, this loafer was quite well up in criminal or legal matters ; when this pressman I knew gave him a cigar and some beer, he

would close his eyes, take a few puffs and begin to give the
details of the finest and strangest criminal cases you could
imagine ; then he'd mention the chief points in the defence
and quote the public prosecutor's speech in reply, after
which he'd pass sentence in the name of the Republic. Then
he'd open his eyes, as if he had just woken up, and growl :
' Lend me five crowns.' Once they put him through a test :
At one sitting he invented twenty-one criminal cases, each
one better than the one before it ; but when he got to the
twenty-second he stopped short and said : ' Wait a bit, this
isn't a case for the petty sessions or even a bench of magistrates ; it'd have to go before a jury ; and I don't do juries.'
You see he was against juries on principle. But to be fair
to him, I must say that the sentences he passed, though a bit
severe, were models of their kind from a legal point of view ;
he particularly prided himself on that.

" When the reporters discovered Havlena and saw that
the cases he supplied them with were not so hackneyed and
dull as those which actually came up before the courts, they
formed a sort of trust. For every case which he thought out,
Havlena got what they called a court fee, consisting of ten
crowns and a cigar, and besides that, two crowns for every
month's imprisonment which he imposed ; you see, the
heavier the sentence, the more difficult the case. The newspaper readers had never before got such a kick out of the
police news as when Havlena was supplying his sham
criminal cases. No, sir, and now the papers aren't nearly as
good as they were in his time ; now it's nothing but politics
and lawsuits—Heaven alone knows who reads the stuff.

" Now one day Havlena thought out a case, which wasn't
by far one of his best, and though up till then none of them
had ever caused any trouble, this time the gaff was blown.
Reduced to its lowest terms, the case was like this : An old
bachelor had a row with a respectable widow who lived

opposite him ; so he got a parrot and trained it up, so that
whenever the lady appeared on her balcony, it screeched out
at the top of its voice : ' You slut ! '   The widow brought an
action against him for defamation of character.   The district
court decided that the defendant, through the agency of his
parrot, had made a public laughing-stock of the prosecutrix,
and in the name of the Republic, sentenced him to fourteen
days' imprisonment with costs.   ' Eleven crowns and a cigar,
please,' said Havlena as a conclusion to the proceedings.

" This particular case appeared in about six newspapers,
although it was written up in various ways.   In one paper
the heading was :   ' Far From The Madding Crowd.'   In
another : ' Landlord and Poor Widow.' A third paper called
it : ' Accusation against Parrot.'   And so on.   But suddenly
all these papers received a communication from the Ministry
of Justice asking for particulars of the district court before
which the charge of defamation of character, reported in
number so-and-so of your esteemed journal, had been tried ;
the verdict and sentence should be appealed against, since
the incriminating words had been uttered, not by the
defendant, but by the parrot ; that it could not be regarded
as proven that the words uttered by the said parrot in-
dubitably referred to the prosecutrix ; that hence the words
in question could not be regarded as defamation of character,
but at the very utmost as disorderly conduct or a breach of
the peace, which could have been dealt with by binding the
defendant over, by duly imposing a fine, or by issuing a court
order for the removal of the bird in question.   The Ministry
of Justice accordingly desired to know which district court
had dealt with the case, in order that it might institute
appropriate inquiries and so forth ; in fact it was a regular
official rumpus.

" ' Good Lord, Havlena, you haven't half landed us in a

mess,' the reporters protested to their retailer. ' Look here, that sentence you passed in the parrot case is illegal.'

" Havlena went as white as a sheet. ' What,' he shouted, ' the sentence *I* passed is illegal. Holy Moses, the Ministry of Justice has got the cheek to tell me that ? Me, Havlena ?' The reporters said they'd never seen a man so offended and angry. ' I'll give them what for,' shouted Havlena, flying into a temper. ' I'll show them whether my verdict's illegal or not ! I'm not going to take this lying down.'—In his vexation and excitement he got terribly drunk ; then he took a sheet of paper and for the benefit of the Ministry of Justice drew up a detailed legal statement to vindicate the verdict ; in it he said by teaching his parrot to insult the lady the defendant had manifested his deliberate intention to insult and disparage her ; that hence this was a clear case of unlawful intent ; that the parrot was not the perpetrator of, but only the instrument for, the offence in question ; and so forth. As a matter of fact, it was the most subtle and brilliant piece of legal reasoning which those reporters had ever seen. Whereupon he signed it with his full name, Václav Havlena, and sent it to the Ministry of Justice. ' That's that,' he said, ' and until the matter's dealt with, I'm not going to give any more judgments ; I must get satisfaction first.'

" As you can imagine, the Ministry of Justice took no notice whatever of Havlena's communication ; meanwhile Havlena went about looking disgruntled and down in the mouth ; he looked seedier than ever and got very thin. When he saw that he had no chance of getting any answer from the Ministry, he quite lost heart ; he would spit silently or talk treason, and at last he declared : ' Just you wait, I'll show 'em yet who's in the right.'

" For two months they saw nothing of him ; then he turned up again, beaming and smirking, and announced :

' Well, I've been served with a writ at last ! Whew, damn
that old woman, I had the deuce of a job before I could
persuade her to do it. You wouldn't believe that an old girl
like that could be so inoffensive ; she made me sign a paper
that whatever happened I'd foot the bill for her. Anyhow,
boys, now it's going to be settled in court.'

" ' What is ? ' the reporters asked.

" ' Why, that affair with the parrot,' said Havlena. ' I
told you I wouldn't let it slide. You see, I bought a parrot
and taught it to say : " You slut ! you wicked old geezer ! "
And a deuce of a job it was too, I tell you. For six weeks I
didn't set foot outside the house and never uttered a word
but : " You slut ! " Anyway, now the parrot says it very
nicely ; the only thing is that the damned stupid bird keeps
on shouting it the whole blessed day ; it just wouldn't get
into the way of only shouting at the woman who lives on the
other side of the yard. She's an old girl who gives music
lessons ; she's seen better days, quite a good sort ; but as
there aren't any other females in the house, I had to pick on
her for the defamation of character. I tell you, it's easy
enough to think out an offence like that, but, holy Moses,
when it comes to committing it, that's a very different thing.
I just couldn't teach that brute of a parrot to call only her
names. It calls every one names. If you ask me, it does
that out of sheer cussedness.'

" Then Havlena had a long drink and went on : ' So I
tried a different wheeze ; whenever the old lady showed her
face at the window or in the yard I opened the window in
double-quick time so as the parrot could shout at her :
" You slut ! You wicked old geezer ! " And I'm blowed
if the old girl didn't start laughing and called over to me :
" Well I never, Mr. Havlena, what a nice little bird you've
got ! " ' Damn the old woman,' growled Mr. Havlena. ' I
had to keep pegging away at her for a fortnight, before she'd

bring an action against me ; but I've got witnesses from all over the house. Aha, and now it's going to be settled in court,' and Havlena rubbed his hands. ' I'll eat my hat if I'm not convicted for defamation of character. Those jacks-in-office won't get much change out of me ! '

" Until the day when the case came on, Mr. Havlena drank like a fish ; he was nervy and restless. In court he was quite the little gentleman ; he made a biting speech against himself, referring to the evidence of all the people in the house that the insult was a disgraceful and flagrant one, and demanded the most exemplary penalty. The magistrate, quite a decent old fellow, stroked his beard and said that he would like to hear the parrot. So he adjourned the proceedings and instructed the defendant at the next hearing to bring the bird with him as an exhibit or, should the need arise, as a witness.

" Mr. Havlena appeared at the next hearing with the parrot in a cage. The parrot goggled its eyes at the frightened lady clerk and began to shriek with all its might : ' You slut ! You wicked old geezer ! '

" ' That's enough,' said the magistrate. ' The evidence of the parrot Lora makes it plain that the expression it used did not refer directly and unequivocally to the prosecutrix."

" The parrot looked at him and yelled : ' You slut ! '— ' But it is obvious,' continued his worship, ' that it makes use of the expression in question toward all persons, irrespective of their sex. Accordingly there is an absence of contumelious intent, Mr. Havlena.'

" Havlena darted up as if he had been stung. ' Your worship,' he protested excitedly, ' the unlawful intent to cause annoyance is shown by the fact that I was in the habit of opening the window which gave access to the prosecutrix for the purpose of causing the parrot to bring her into contempt.'

" ' That's a moot point,' said his worship. ' The opening of the window possibly indicates some degree of unlawful intent, but in itself it is not a contumelious action. I cannot convict you for opening the window from time to time. You cannot prove that your parrot had the prosecutrix in mind, Mr. Havlena.'

" ' But *I* had her in mind,' urged Havlena in self-defence.

" ' We have no evidence as to that,' demurred the magistrate. ' Nobody heard you utter the incriminating expression. It's no use, Mr. Havlena, I shall have to acquit you.' Whereupon he pronounced judgment accordingly.

" ' And I beg to give notice of appeal against the acquittal,' Havlena burst forth, snatched up the cage containing the bird and rushed out of court, nearly weeping with rage.

" After that they used to come across him here and there, fuddled and devil-may-care. ' Do you call that justice ? ' he would scream. ' Is there any chance for a man to get his rights anywhere at all ? But I won't let matters rest there. I'll have it brought up before the high court. I've got to get my own back for the way I've been made a fool of, even if I have to spend the rest of my life bringing actions. I'm not fighting for my cause, but for justice.'

" I don't exactly know what happened in the appeal court ; all I know is that Mr. Havlena's appeal against his acquittal was dismissed. Then Havlena vanished into thin air ; there were people who said they'd seen him loitering about the streets like a lost soul and muttering something to himself ; I have also heard that to this very day the Ministry of Justice still receives several times a year, a long and furious petition headed : *Defamation of character committed by a parrot*. But Mr. Havlena has, once and for all, stopped supplying police-news reporters with cases ; most likely because his faith in law and order has been rudely shaken."

The Needle

*   *   *

" I'VE NEVER had any dealings with law-courts," said Mr. Kostelecký, " but I must say that what I like about them is their tremendous fairness and the speechifying and the fuss they often make, and they don't mind if it's all over a mere nothing. It sort of makes you feel you really can put your trust in law and order. If Justice has got a pair of scales in her hands, they may as well be like an apothecary's, and if she holds a sword, it may as well have a sharp edge. That reminds me of an affair that happened in our street.

" There was a house-porter's wife, a Mrs. Mašková who bought some rolls in a shop, and while she was munching one, suddenly something pricked the roof of her mouth ; so she shoved her fingers down her throat and fished out a needle that had got stuck in her palate. It wasn't until a little later that she had a fright—' Good gracious me, I might have swallowed the needle and then it would have pricked a hole in my stomach. Why, it might have been the death of me, and I'm not going to put up with that. We shall have to find out who was the brute who put the needle into that roll.'—So off· she went and took the needle and what was left of the roll to the police.

" The police cross-examined the man who'd sold the roll and they cross-examined the baker who'd baked it, but of course neither of them recognized the needle. Then the police started court proceedings, because, you see, it was a case of causing bodily harm. The magistrate, who performed his official duties thoroughly and conscientiously, again cross-examined the man who'd sold the roll and the baker who'd baked it ; they both swore blind that the needle couldn't have got into the roll while it was in their hands. The magistrate called on the man who'd sold the roll and satisfied himself that there weren't any needles in the shop. Then he called on the baker to see how the rolls were baked ; he sat all night in the bakehouse and saw how the dough was kneaded, how they let it rise, how they heated the oven and shaped the rolls and put them into the oven until they were done to a turn. In this way he satisfied himself that no needles are used in the baking of rolls. You wouldn't believe what a fine job it is to bake rolls, and especially to bake bread. My poor old dad had a bakery, so I know all about it. You see, in making bread, you've got two or three important secrets which are practically holy. The first secret is how to make the yeast ; you have to leave it in the trough and then there's a sort of mysterious change takes place under the lid ; you have to wait until the flour and water turn into live yeast. Then the dough is made and mixed with what they call a mash-ladle ; and that's a job that looks like a religious dance or something of that sort. Then they cover it with a cloth and let the dough rise ; that's another mysterious change, when the dough grandly rises and bulges, and you mustn't lift the cloth to peep under- neath—I tell you, it's as fine and strange as the process of birth. I've always had a feeling that there was something of a woman about that trough. And the third secret is the actual baking, the thing that happens to the soft and pale dough in the oven. Ye gods, when you take out the loaf, all golden and russet, and it smells more delicious than a baby, it's such a marvel—why, I think that when these three changes are going on, they ought to ring a bell in the bakeries, the same as they do in church at the elevation of the Host.

" But to come back to my story, the magistrate was now at his wits' end. Not that he intended to let the matter drop, oh dear no! So he took the needle and sent it to the Chemical Institute, so that they could discover there whether the needle was in the roll before it was baked or afterwards ; this magistrate, I may say, was particularly keen on scientific reports. Now at that time there was a certain Professor Uher at the Chemical Institute, a very learned man with whiskers. When he received the needle, he began to swear furiously about the way the law-courts bothered him with all kinds of damn-fool inquiries : only the other day, he complained, they'd sent him some entrails which were so decayed that even the dissection man couldn't stand it, and anyway, what had the Chemical Institute to do with needles ? But then somehow he changed his mind and it began to interest him, the scientific side of it, of course. Why, he said to himself, it may be that the needle really does undergo some changes when it gets into the dough or when it's baked inside it ; acids or something of that sort are formed when the dough ferments and then some more when it's baked, and perhaps that damages or corrodes the surface of the needle a bit ; if so, it could be discovered by a microscopic examination. So he set about the job.

" First of all he bought several hundred needles, some quite clean and others more or less rusty, and began to bake rolls in the Chemical Institute. At the first experiment he put the needles into the yeast to find out what effect the fermentation had on them. At the second experiment he put them into the freshly kneaded dough. At the third, into the rising dough. At the fourth, into the risen dough. Then he placed them there immediately before baking. Then during the baking. After that he shoved them into the rolls while they were still warm ; and finally, into the rolls when they were finished. Then he did the whole series of experiments once more, just to check his results. In fact, for a whole fortnight they did nothing else at the Chemical Institute but bake rolls with needles ; the professor, the lecturer, four assistants and a lab.-boy day after day kneaded dough, put rolls into the oven, baked them, whereupon they examined the various needles microscopically and compared the results. That meant another week's work, but in the end they discovered beyond the possibility of any doubt that the needle in question had been shoved into the roll after it had been baked, because microscopically it corresponded exactly to the experimental needles which had been put into the rolls when they were finished.

" On the strength of this report the magistrate decided that the needle must have got into the roll either in the shop where it was sold or else on the way from the bake-house to the· shop. At this point the baker suddenly remembered, why, hang it all, that's the day I gave an apprentice the sack, the errand boy who used to take the rolls round in a basket. So they summoned the boy and he admitted that he'd put the needle in the roll because he wanted to get his own back. As the boy was under age, he was only bound over, but the baker had to pay a fine of fifty crowns, because he was responsible for what his employees did. So there you have an example of how thorough and fair justice is.

" But there's another side to the story. I don't know what it is, but we men are somehow eager to show what we can do or else it's just cussedness or something ; anyway, once they started baking experimental rolls in the Chemical Institute, those chemist chaps took into their heads that they must bake them properly. At first they were all anyhow, they hadn't risen as they ought to and they didn't look right ; but the more of them they baked, the better they got. Then they sprinkled poppy-seeds, salt and carraway-seeds on them, and twisted them into such pretty shapes that they were a treat to look at. The end of it was that those chemist chaps boasted that there was no place in the whole of Prague where rolls were as fine and crisp and tasty as the ones they baked in the Chemical Institute."

" You may call it cussedness, Mr. Kostelecký," said Mr. Lelek, " but if you ask me, it's more like a sporting instinct : you know, it's when a man's anxious to do his level best.   A real sportsman doesn't do it for the sake of the result, which may not, in itself, be worth the trouble ; but he does it because it's like playing a game and exerting yourself of your own accord.   I can explain what I mean by a single example, although you may say it's all rot and is quite beside the point.

" Anyway, when I used to be in our counting-house and had to do the half-yearly balances, it sometimes happened that I couldn't make the figures tally ; for instance, there were exactly three hellers we couldn't account for.   Of course, it would have been the easiest thing in the world for me to make up the three hellers out of my own pocket, but that wouldn't have been fair, you see, from a cashier's point of view, it wouldn't have been sportsmanlike ; the thing was, to find out in which of the fourteen thousand or so entries the error was.   And I don't mind telling you that before the job started, I always looked forward to the chance that some such error would crop up.

" And when it did, I'd stay sometimes all night in the counting-house, pile up all the ledgers in front of me, and then I'd get to work.   You know, it's a funny thing, but I looked upon those columns of figures, not as numbers, but as things.   Sometimes I'd imagine that I was climbing up on those figures, as if they were a steep rock, or that I was lowering myself on them into a pit, as if they were a ladder. At other times I felt like a hunter who was working his way through a brushwood of figures to catch a rare and timid animal—that was those three hellers.   Or I would fancy that I was a detective on the watch in the dark round the corner ;

thousands of figures pass by, but I'm waiting to collar that crook, that criminal, that tiny error in the accounts. Sometimes I thought I was sitting on the bank of a river with a rod and line, angling ; suddenly I give the line a jerk, and now I've got you, you brute. But more often than not, I liked to think I was a hunter trudging up and down through the wet thickets ; I felt as thrilled and elated, as jaunty and eager as if I was enjoying some adventure or other. I tell you, I would spend the whole night chasing after those three hellers ; and when I'd caught them, it never occurred to me that it was only a paltry three hellers ; it was nothing short of a trophy, and I went home so victorious and in such high spirits that it's a wonder I didn't go to bed with my boots on. And there you have the whole thing in a nut-shell."

The Stamp Collection

★　★　★

"THERE'S NO getting away from it," said old Mr. Karas. "If a man were to rummage in his past, he'd find material in it for a whole different set of lives. One day, either by mistake, or because he felt inclined to, he chose just one of them and went on with it to the end ; but the worst of it is, that those other lives, the ones he might have lived, are not entirely dead. And sometimes it happens that you feel a pain in them, like a leg that has been cut off.

"When I was a boy of about ten, I began to collect stamps; my father didn't altogether approve of it ; he thought it'd make me neglect my lessons, but I had a chum, Lojzik Čepelka, and we used to share our passion for foreign stamps. Lojzik's father used to play a barrel-organ, and he was an untidy lad with freckles, a regular ragamuffin, but I was fond of him, in the way that schoolboys are fond of their chum. You know, I'm an old man ; I've had a wife and children, but I must say that none of our feelings are finer than friendship. But you're only capable of it when you're young ; later on, you get sort of crusty and selfish. A friendship of the sort I mean springs simply and solely from enthusiasm and admiration, from excess of vitality, from abundance and overflow of emotion ; you've got so much of it, that you simply have to give it away to somebody. My father was a lawyer, the chief man among the local bigwigs, a most dignified and severe person, and I had chummed up with Lojzik, whose father was a drunken organ-grinder and his mother a downtrodden laundress, and yet I venerated and idolized Lojzik, because he was smarter than myself, because he could shift for himself and was as plucky as they make them, because he had freckles on his nose and could throw stones left-handed—in fact, I can't remember all the things that made me so attached to him ; but it was certainly the closest attachment I have ever had.

" And so Lojzik was my trusty comrade when I began to collect stamps. I suppose that the craze for collecting things must be a survival of an instinct dating back to the times when every male collected the heads of his enemies, the spoils of war, bearskins, stags' antlers, and, in fact, anything that he could capture as booty. But a stamp collection possesses one quality which makes it a perpetual adventure ; it some-how excites you to touch a bit of some distant country, such as Bhutan, Bolivia or the Cape of Good Hope ; it brings you into a sort of personal and intimate touch with these foreign countries. So there is something about stamp-collecting which suggests travel by land and sea, and deeds of derring-do, in general. It's very much the same as the crusades.

" As I was saying, my father didn't exactly approve of it ; as a rule, fathers don't approve of it, if their sons do some-thing different from what they themselves have done : as a matter of fact, I'm just the same with my own sons. This business of being a father is a sort of mixed feeling, there's a great deal of affection in it, but there's also a certain pre-judice, mistrust, hostility or whatever you may choose to call it ; the more affection you have for your children, the more there is of this other feeling. Anyway, I had to hide my stamp collection in the attic, so that my father couldn't catch me with it ; in the attic there was an old chest, a sort of flour-bin, and we used to crawl into it like a couple of mice to have a look at each other's stamps. Look here, this is a Netherlands, this is an Egyptian, this is Sverige or Sweden. And because we had to hide our treasures like that, there was something deliciously sinful about it. The way I got hold of those stamps was also an adventurous business ; I used to go round to families I knew and those I didn't, and beg and pray of them to let me soak the stamps off their old letters. Now and then I came across people who'd got drawers crammed full of old papers stored away, in an attic or a writing-table ; those were my most delightful hours when, sitting on the floor, I sorted out those dusty piles of litter to try and find stamps I hadn't already got—you see, I was silly enough not to collect duplicates, and when I happened to come across an old Lombardy or one of those tiny German states or free cities, why, the thrill I had was perfectly agonizing—every vast happiness has a sweet pang about it. And in the meantime Lojzik was waiting for me outside, and when at last I crept out, I whispered right in the doorway, ' Lojzik, Lojzik, I found a Hanover there ! '— ' Have you got it ? '—' Yes.' And away we ran with our booty, home to our treasure-chest.

" In our town there were factories which turned out all sorts of trash, jute, calico, cotton, and shoddy wool—the rubbish that we produce specially for the coloured races all over the world. They used to let me ransack their waste-paper baskets, and that was my happiest hunting-ground ; there I came across stamps from Siam and South Africa, China, Liberia, Afghanistan, Borneo, Brazil, New Zealand, India, the Congo—I wonder whether the mere sound of the names gives you the same sense of mystery and glamour as it does me. Good heavens, what joy, what frantic joy I felt when I found a stamp from, say, the Straits Settlements, or Korea or Nepal or New Guinea or Sierra Leone or Madagascar ! I tell you, that particular rapture can be realized only by a hunter or a treasure-seeker or an archæologist who's doing excavations. To seek and to find—that's the greatest thrill and satisfaction which a man can get out of life. Everybody ought to seek something ; if not stamps, then truth or golden ferns or at least, stone arrow-heads and ash-trays.

"Well, those were the happiest years of my life, my friendship with Lojzik and stamp-collecting. Then I had scarlet fever and they wouldn't let Lojzik come to see me, but he used to stand in the passage and whistle so that I could hear him. One day they must have taken their eyes off me or something ; at all events, I got out of bed and slipped upstairs to the attic to have a look at my stamps. I was so feeble that I could hardly lift the lid of the trunk. But the trunk was empty ; the box containing the stamps was gone.

"I can't describe to you how distressed and horror-stricken I was. I think I must have stood there as if I'd been turned to stone, and I couldn't even cry, there was such a lump in my throat. First of all, it was appalling to me that my stamps, my greatest joy, were gone—but what was more appalling was that Lojzik, the only friend I had, must have stolen them while I was ill. I felt overwhelmed, dismayed, dumbfounded, stunned—you know, it's amazing how much a child can suffer. How I got out of that attic, I don't know ; but after that I had high fever again and during my clearer moments I pondered in despair. I never said a word about this to my father or my aunt—I had no mother—I knew that they simply wouldn't understand me, and through that I became rather estranged from them ; from that time onwards my feelings for them ceased to be close and childlike. Lojzik's treachery affected me terribly, it was the first time anyone had played me false. ' A beggar,' I said to myself, ' Lojzik's a beggar and that's why he steals ; it serves me right for chumming up with a beggar.' And this hardened my heart ; it was then I began to draw a distinction between one person and another—I forfeited my state of social innocence ; but at the time I didn't realize what a shock it had been to me and how much damage it had caused.

" When I had got over my fever, I also got over my distress at the loss of my stamp collection, though my heart still ached when I saw that Lojzik had now found new friends ; but when he came running up to me, rather sheepishly because it was so long since we'd seen each other, I said to him in a curt, grown-up tone : ' You sling your hook, I've finished with you.' Lojzik turned red and presently replied : ' All right, then.' And from that time onward he hated me as thoroughly as the underdog can hate.

" Well, that was the incident which affected my whole life. The world I lived in was, so to speak, desecrated ; I lost my faith in people ; I learned how to hate and despise. After that I never had a friend ; and when I grew up, I began to assume that because I was by myself, I needed nobody and would show favour to nobody. Then I discovered that nobody liked me ; I used to put this down to the fact that I despised affection and was proof against all sentimentality. And so I became an aloof and purposeful man, very fussy about myself, very punctilious, and the kind of person who always wants to do the right thing ; I was cantankerous and harsh towards my subordinates ; I did not love the woman I married ; I brought up my children to obey and fear me, and by my industry and sense of duty I gained quite a reputation. Such was my life, my whole life ; I attended to nothing except my duty. When my time comes the newspapers will say what valuable work I did and what an exemplary character I had. But if people only knew how much solitude, mistrust and self-will there is about it all.

" Three years ago my wife died. I never admitted it to myself or to anybody else, but I was terribly upset ; and in my distress I rummaged about among all sorts of family keepsakes which had been left by my father and mother :

o

photographs, letters, my old school exercise-books—I felt like choking when I saw how carefully my stern father had arranged and kept them ; I think that, after all, he must have been fond of me. The cupboard in the attic was filled with these things, and at the bottom of a drawer was a box sealed with my father's seals; when I opened it I discovered the stamp collection I had made fifty years earlier.

" I'm not going to keep anything back from you : I burst into tears and I took the box into my room like a man who has found a treasure. So *that's* what happened, suddenly flashed across my mind ; while I was ill, somebody must have found my stamp collection and my father confiscated it, so that I should not neglect my lessons. He oughtn't to have done it, but it was all because of his concern and affection for me ; I don't know how it was, but I began to feel sorry for him and for myself.

" And then I remembered : so Lojzik never stole my stamps. Good heavens, how I had wronged him ! Again I saw the freckled and untidy urchin before me, and I wondered what had become of him and whether he was still alive. I tell you, I felt so wretched and ashamed when I looked back on it all. Because of a single false suspicion I had lost my only friend ; because of that I had wasted my childhood. Because of that I had begun to despise the lower orders ; because of that I had been so self-opinionated; because of that I never became attached to anyone. Because of that the very sight of a postage-stamp always made me feel annoyed and disgusted. Because of that I never wrote to my wife, either before or after our marriage, and I explained this away by pretending to be above what I chose to call gush ; and my wife felt this keenly. Because of that I was harsh and aloof. Because of that, only because of that, I had so fine a career and performed my duties in such an exemplary manner.

" I saw my whole life afresh ; suddenly it seemed a different life, was the thought which struck me. If that hadn't happened I should have been so full of enthusiasm and dash, affection, chivalry, wit and resourcefulness, strange and unruly things of that sort—why, good heavens, I might have been almost anything else, an explorer or an actor or a soldier ! Why, I might have felt some affection for my fellow-men, I might have drunk with them, understood them, oh, there's no knowing what I mightn't have done. I felt as if ice were thawing inside me. I went through the collection, stamp by stamp ; they were all there, Lombardy, Cuba, Siam, Hanover, Nicaragua, the Philippines, all the places which I had wanted to go to and which I shall now never see. On each of these stamps there was a scrap of something which might have been and never was. I sat brooding over them all night and took stock of my life. I realized that it had been an artificial and impersonal life, which did not belong to me, and that my proper life had never come into existence." Mr. Karas shook his head sadly. " When I consider all I might have been, and how I wronged Lojzik——"

Father Voves, on hearing these words, looked very downcast and forlorn ; most likely he had remembered something in his own life. " Mr. Karas," he said pityingly, " don't think about it ; it's no use, you can't put it right now, you can't make a fresh start——"

" No," sighed Mr. Karas with a slight flush. " But you know, anyhow—anyhow, I've started collecting stamps again."

An Ordinary Murder

*   *   *

"I'VE OFTEN wondered," said Hanák, "why we look upon unjust treatment as worse than pretty well anything that can happen to a man. For instance, if we saw one single innocent man sent to prison, we should be more upset and worried by it than by thousands of people living in misery and distress. I have seen misery so awful that any prison is sheer luxury compared with it ; and yet the worst possible misery doesn't shock us as much as unjust treatment. I suppose there's a sort of instinct for justice implanted within us, and our feelings of guilt and innocence, right and justice are just as primitive, ruthless and profound as love and hunger.

"Take this example : I was at the front for four years, like most of you were ; we won't tell each other what we saw there, but you'll agree with me that the likes of us got accustomed to pretty well anything—to dead bodies, for instance. I've seen hundreds and hundreds of young fellows dead and sometimes, as you know, their corpses were ghastly sights ; and I don't mind telling you that after a time they meant no more to me than if they were so many bundles of old rags, as long as they didn't stink. All I said to myself was, if you get out of this beastly mess safe and sound, nothing's going to upset you for the rest of your life.

"About six months after the war, I was at Slatina where my home is ; one morning somebody tapped at my window and shouted : 'Mr. Hanák, come and have a look, Mrs. Turková has been killed.' Now this Mrs. Turková kept a small shop where she sold stationery and thread ; nobody had ever bothered about her, and it was only now and then that somebody came into that small shop of hers for a hank of thread or some Christmas cards. At the back of the shop there was a door with glass panels leading into a sort of kitchen, where she slept ; this door had curtains on it, and when the shop-bell rang, Mrs. Turková would peep through these curtains from the kitchen to see who it was, then she'd wipe her hands on her apron and shuffle into the shop. ' Yes, what is it ? ' she'd ask suspiciously ; the customer would feel like an intruder there and he'd do his best to get out again as quickly as he could. It was just as if you were to lift up a stone and underneath it, in a damp hole, a lonely and frightened beetle was scurrying about ; then you'd put the stone back, so as not to disturb the repulsive creature.

" So when I heard the news, I rushed off to have a look, I suppose just out of vulgar curiosity. There was a regular swarm of people in front of Mrs. Turková's shop ; but the local constable let me go in, because he looked upon me as a sort of learned gent. The bell tinkled just as at any other time, but at that moment the clear and eager sound it made gave me quite a creepy feeling ; I couldn't help thinking that it was quite out of place there. At the foot of the doorway to the kitchen Mrs. Turková was lying with her face to the ground, and under her head there was a pool of blood which by now had turned nearly black ; the white hair on the nape of her neck was all matted with blood which had left dark stains. And at that moment I suddenly had a feeling that I had never experienced during the war—I was horrified by a dead body.

" It's a funny thing, but I've nearly forgotten about the war ; in fact, everybody's forgetting about it gradually, and I suppose that's why, sooner or later, there'll have to be another war. But never will I forget that murdered old woman who wasn't of much account while she was here, that petty shopkeeper who couldn't even sell a picture-postcard without muddling things up. A murdered person is not the same thing as a dead person ; there's a terrible secret about someone who's been murdered. For the life of me I couldn't understand why Mrs. Turková of all people had been murdered, that commonplace and dingy old woman to whom nobody had ever given a second thought ; and how it had come about that she was lying there so grimly with a policeman bending over her, while outside, crowds of people were pushing to try and catch a glimpse of her. What it came to was that the poor creature had never attracted such attention as now that she was lying there with her face in a pool of clotted blood. It was as if she had suddenly acquired a strange and terrible importance. Never, from one year's end to another, had I noticed how she was dressed and what she really looked like ; but now I seemed to be looking at her through a glass that made things look enormously and horribly bigger. There was a slipper on one foot, the other slipper had been taken off and you could see where the stocking had been patched at the heel—I could see every stitch, and there was something dreadful about it, I thought, as if even the poor, wretched stocking had been murdered, too. One hand was clutching at the floor ; it looked as withered and powerless as a bird's claw; but the most horrible part of it all was the tuft of grey hair in the nape of the corpse's neck, because it was plaited so carefully and shone like old pewter among the smears of clotted blood. I had a feeling as if I'd never seen anything more pitiful than that soiled mesh of hair. One patch of blood had dried behind her ear; a small silver ear-ring with a blue stone was glistening above it. I couldn't stand the sight any longer—my legs trembled. ' My God ! ' I said.

" The policeman, who was in the kitchen looking for something on the ground, stood up and looked at me ; he was pale, like a man who is on the point of fainting.

" ' Man alive,' I gasped, ' weren't you at the front ? '

" ' Yes,' said the policeman hoarsely. ' But this—this is different. Look at that,' he suddenly added, and pointed to the curtains on the door ; they were crumpled and stained, evidently the murderer had wiped his hands on them. ' Good God ! ' I gasped ; I don't know what there was so unbearably ghastly about it—whether it was the idea of the hands, sticky with blood, or that even the curtains, the neat clean curtains had become a victim of the crime.— Anyhow, I don't know ; but at that moment a canary in the kitchen started warbling and came out with a long trill. Well, that was really more than I could stand ; I just bolted out of the shop in sheer horror, and I believe I was even paler than the policeman.

" Then I sat down in our yard on the axle of an open cart and tried to collect my thoughts. ' You fool,' I said to myself, ' you coward, why, it's just an ordinary murder ! Haven't you ever seen blood before ? Haven't you been splashed with your own blood, like a pig with mire ? Haven't you shouted to your men to hurry up and dig a pit for a hundred and thirty corpses ? A hundred and thirty corpses, side by side, that makes quite a longish row, even if you put them as close together as tiles on a roof—you walked alongside them, smoked a cigarette and yelled at the troops : *Now then, get a move on there, get a move on, don't be all night over it.* Haven't you seen plenty of corpses, plenty of corpses—— ?

" ' Yes, that's right enough,' I said to myself, ' I've seen plenty of corpses, but I've never seen just a single corpse ; I've never knelt down beside it to look into its face and touch its hair.' A corpse is horribly quiet, you must

be alone with it . . . and not even breathe . . . if you want
to understand it. Every one of those hundred and thirty
would have made an effort to say to you : ' They've killed
me, sir ; look at my hands—they're a man's hands ! '—
But we all turned away from those corpses ; when we had to
fight, we couldn't listen to the dead. By God, it'd be a
good thing if people—boys, women and children—were to
swarm like bees round every dead man, so that they could
catch at least a glimpse and shudder—at least a glimpse of a
foot in a shoe or of blood-stained hair. Then perhaps such
things wouldn't happen ; then they couldn't happen.

" And I saw my mother buried ; she looked so solemn, so
tranquil and dignified in her shapely coffin. She was strange,
but she was not terrible. But this, this is something else
than death ; anyone who is murdered is not dead ; they
lament, as if they were screaming with pain, extreme and
unbearable pain. The policeman and I, we knew it ; we
knew that the shop was haunted. And something began to
dawn upon me. I don't know whether we've got a soul ;
but there are immortal things within us, such as the impulse
towards justice. I'm not a bit better than anyone else ; but
there is something within me which doesn't belong to me
alone,—it's a vague feeling that there is such a thing as a
strict and powerful ordinance. I know I'm putting this
clumsily ; but at that moment I knew what is meant by
crime and by outrage against God. You know, a murdered
person is like a defiled and devastated temple."

" And by the way," remarked Mr. Dobeš, " did they
catch the fellow who killed the old woman ? "
" Yes," continued Mr. Hanák, " and I saw him, two days
later, when the police were taking him out of the shop, where
they'd been cross-questioning him on the scene of the crime,
as it's called. I don't suppose I saw him for longer than

five seconds, but again I seemed to be looking through a lens that made things monstrously bigger. He was a young fellow with handcuffs on and he was hurrying forward at such a devil of a rate that the policemen could hardly keep up with him. His nose was sweating and his bulging eyes were blinking with fear—you could see that he was scared out of his wits like a rabbit being vivisected. I'll never forget his face as long as I live. After that encounter I felt very glum and out of sorts. Now they're going to try him, I thought to myself, they'll mess about with him for a few months and then sentence him to death. The end of it was that I saw I really felt sorry for him, and I should have almost felt relieved if he had somehow managed to wriggle out of it. Not that he was attractive to look at, it was more the other way about ; but I saw him too close up—I saw him blinking with fright. Damn it all, I'm not a tender-hearted sort of chap, but as close up as all that, he wasn't a murderer, he was just a man. I must say, I didn't pretend to understand it myself ; I didn't know what I should have done, if I had had to try him ; but it all made me feel as wretched as if my own soul wanted saving."

GEORGE ALLEN & UNWIN LTD

London: 40 Museum Street, W.C.1

Auckland: P.O. Box 36013, Northcote Central, N.4
Bombay: 15 Graham Road, Ballard Estate, Bombay 1
Barbados: P.O. Box 222, Bridgetown
Buenos Aires: Escritorio 454–459, Florida 165
Calcutta: 17 Chittaranjan Avenue, Calcutta 13
Cape Town: 68 Shortmarket Street
Hong Kong: 105 Wing On Mansion, 26 Hancow Road, Kowloon
Ibadan: P.O. Box 62
Karachi: Karachi Chambers, McLeod Road
Madras: Mohan Mansions, 38c Mount Road, Madras 6
Mexico: Villalongin 32–10, Piso, Mexico 5, D.F.
Nairobi: P.O. Box 4536
New Delhi: 13–14 Asaf Ali Road, New Delhi 1
Ontario: 81 Curlew Drive, Don Mills
Rio de Janeiro: Caixa Postal 2537–Zc–00
São Paulo: Caixa Postal 8675
Singapore: 36c Prinsep Street, Singapore 7
Sydney, N.S.W.: Bradbury House, 55 York Street
Tokyo: P.O. Box 26, Kamata

LETTERS FROM ENGLAND

Writing thirty years ago, Karel Čapek produced a very brief but acutely observant account of his travels in England and Scotland. It is remarkable in that the things which he found execrable—English Sundays, English cooking, traffic jams and Glasgow— are still today the objects of articles and excited comment. When he writes "Every Englishman wears a macintosh and has a cap on his head and newspaper in his hand. As for the English-woman she carries a macintosh or a tennis racket", can we doubt that he reaches into the character of the English race at its most stable point?

It was not only our habits and surroundings which evoked Čapek's reflections. He visited several of the literary figures of the time. His summaries of Galsworthy, Chesterton, and Wells are not to be bettered. He was scared of Bernard Shaw and writes "he looks half like God and half like a very malicious sartyr". Illustrations and text are imbued with Čapek's sense of fun and throughout the book there is the most delightful play between exaggerated comment, irony and amused satire. In the same spirit the reviewer in *Punch* wrote "No better book than *Letters from England* has been written about our race since Tacitus' 'Germania'."

Long out-of-print, it has now been republished by Allen & Unwin.

"He is an artist of delicate wit and infinite suggestive-ness . . . Mr. Selver's part in retaining the racy vigour of the Czech cannot be too highly praised."—*The Times*.

"This is a delightful book. We can enjoy this light-hearted record of things done, things seen, and things invented . . . It has the most delicious drawings by the author."—*The Observer*.

"He can be droll and mocking without malice, and he would indeed be a galled jade of an Englishman whose withers were wrung by his satire . . . cleverness on every page."—*Country Life*.

Crown 8vo. Illustrated.

KAREL ČAPEK

I HAD A DOG AND A CAT

You may have read a lot about dogs and cats, but with Čapek's *I Had a Dog and a Cat* you can hardly fail to realize that you are in the presence of one of the kindest and most civilized of human minds that the world has given us. These lovely pages will be a delight to those who have ever lived with dogs and cats and even to those who from time to time in their harassed lives have found themselves watching a dog or a cat in their mysterious ways. What is so unforgettable about the discourses and homilies is that they make you feel how much of life is revealed in these eternal companions of man, how much man reveals himself in this companionship, how much they form a part even of our national life. There are pictures by Karel and Josef Čapek. Their charm and happy humour make the tragedies which have recently closed over these two brothers still more poignant.

Crown 8vo. Illustrated.

APOCRYPHAL STORIES

This collection contains twenty-nine short sketches of famous characters from Prometheus to Napoleon, including several biblical figures and a few well-known characters from literature such as Hamlet, Don Juan and Juliet. Some of the stories are frankly amusing, others rather moving—all have the unexpected twist in them which one has come to expect of the genius of Čapek. They are told in ordinary, everyday dialogue, so effective because of its unexpectedness. One of the charms of reading Čapek is to see his genius at play with so many and varied subjects, and here, in the famous figures of history and literature, his elfin fantasy will delight us as it has done so often before.

Large Crown 8vo.

GEORGE ALLEN & UNWIN LTD